KARA KEEP

WILLIAM BUCKEL

iUniverse, Inc.
Bloomington

Kara Keep

iUniverse books may be ordered through booksellers or by contacting:

iUniverse
1663 Liberty Drive
Bloomington, IN 47403
www.iuniverse.com
1-800-Authors (1-800-288-4677)

ISBN: 978-1-4502-9114-9 (sc)
ISBN: 978-1-4502-8756-2 (ebook)

Printed in the United States of America

iUniverse rev. date: 01/27/2011

For Christina and the family in British Columbia.

Authors Notes

The years 800 to 900 A.D. were exciting years as man in Northern Europe set sail and explored the earth. Harbours were built and trade ships sailed from country to country sharing their wares.

The increase in travel brought with it raiders, the most successful being the Vikings. From 800 A.D. onward they made several attempts to conquer Britain but did not fully succeed until 1016 A.D. ruling the country for twenty five years.

This story is based on the life and times of three generations of women during those years. It was written as a Fiction adventure story from a woman's perspective. This was a time before spoke wheeled carriages and laced hankies. It was a time before the side saddle was invented so women rode as men did.

It was also a time when women of wealth came into being due to inheritance, intelligence, or both. They were also romantic times as true knights had not yet departed, they still walked the earth.

Acknowledgements

I would like to thank Denise Matte-Reece for her support and assistance in the writing of this novel. Her help with female roles and characterization in general was invaluable with this and other projects as well.

The people in our lives that are there whenever we need them are also the ones we forget and take for granted the most. This time I did not.

PART ONE

AMANDA

CHAPTER I

It was autumn, a time when leaves turned red and old people died. Or so mother used to say. But then she died, not old at all. Mother also used to say that premonition was born of instinct not acknowledged any more, that we barely use our instincts at all.

Amanda remembered her mother's words as a messenger galloped his horse through the castle gates. Anxiety welled inside making her tremble. She tried to discern whether those feelings were born of fear or excitement but could not.

"What is wrong Amanda?" asked her maidservant Clorisa.

"The rider. I felt a chill when he rode through the front gate."

"I'll make you some herb tea. You missed breakfast again. It makes you edgy."

Amanda watched the messenger walk from the stables toward the castle door.

"If the messenger is here to see me then send him to the study please."

Amanda sat behind the oak desk as the messenger approached and slammed his fist over his heart in salute. His left hand held the hilt of his broadsword as he stood at attention awaiting a cue to speak.

"Yes soldier, have you a message for me?" asked Amanda.

"Your father requests your immediate presence at Dorville on an urgent matter."

Amanda waited for more but the young man had nothing else to say. She was afraid to ask but finally did.

"My father. Is he well?"

"Yes he looked to be in good health when he dispatched me."

"What of my brother?"

"Also in good health as far as I know."

"My father gave you no further information?"

"None my lady. Only that the matter was urgent and immediate."

"You have had long ride so go to the kitchen for something and tell them I sent you."

"Thank you my lady."

At least her family was well. Amanda went to Clorisa telling her to make haste and ready to leave.

"What is it about?" asked Clorisa.

"I have no idea. Father gave the messenger no letter and no more information than simply to come to Dorville immediately."

"I don't like the sounds of that. He always sends a letter."

Accompanied by four guards and the messenger, Amanda rode through the front gate, Clorisa at her side.

The ride to Dorville would take almost two days making a stopover at Wendell Cross a necessity. Her father had been negotiating a peace treaty with ambassadors from Wildemar a land to the north. She wondered if talks had failed and war was about to break out. Her father would normally have sent a letter or even entrusted the messenger with more information; it must be a matter of extreme urgency.

The inn at Wendell Cross was alive with screams and shouts as men drank after a hard day in the fields. The tone quickly changed when soldiers guarding nobility entered. The women were eyed but heads quickly dropped, no one testing her armed escorts. The barkeep readied rooms while his wife prepared a meal. The soldiers requested a table and stood guard as the women ate. Amanda and Clorisa retired for the night, a soldier guarding their door.

Amanda resented having a soldier standing at her door: she'd been raised in the area, played with friends in the village, and went to school nearby. Having inherited her mother's sizable estate had however changed her life.

She was a target in more ways than one.

Wealth and title made the guard a necessity as kidnap and ransom was a possibility that could not be ignored. Her father would insist on more if he was present.

The next day the sunset behind Dorville castle as Amanda rode through the open gates. She walked to the front door where a butler conveyed a message to proceed to the drawing room where her father was awaiting her arrival.

"Good day father. I will return as soon as I have freshened up. It's been a long ride," said Amanda.

"No you had better hear this from me as rumours abound throughout the castle," said Winfred, her father.

Amanda noticed he had that stern look on his face, the one he'd had when he told her of her mother's death; the tragic look that forewarned of ill news to follow. Amanda's face flushed and a part of her wanted to run before she heard more.

"What is it? Where is Andrew?" asked Amanda.

"Andrew is making final arrangements regarding our pact with Duke Huxley. Your marriage to the duke is part of our arrangement. Half the income from your lands and taxes will go to the duke after your marriage," said Winfred.

"What marriage? When? Where?"

"He is sending an escort for you as we speak. You will be wed at his castle the day of your arrival."

"Father I am self sufficient and need no man to look after me. I have inherited my mother's lands and her role here. Who will manage the estates?" said Amanda.

"You will with your brother's help. Unrest in the north threatens our country. Duke Huxley is all that separates the northern tribes from us. We have made a pact which includes the King and you are part of it. A great part of it, may I add.

"The king's treasury is almost empty and one of his greatest costs is that frontier fortress. He has been troubled by raiders along all his shores and needs further funds to defend those. He wants you to establish some sort of business venture that would turn the north from loss to profit as your mother did here.

"He'll stand behind you as much as possible but understand he will not interfere in a man's private affairs. In other words do not provoke the duke my dear. You are known for your whit and quick tongue but silence might be a virtue with this man." said Winfred.

"Then I have no choice?" said Amanda.

"It has always been the duty of nobility to serve their country even in the bedroom. Your mother was part of an alliance before you."

"Yes but you knew and loved each other. I do not know Huxley or anything about him," said Amanda.

"All I know is that his name is Brand Huxley as it appears on the documents he signed. I know he has the ear of the King and he is a legend in the north. He fights at the head of his army and has kept heathen tribes from our borders."

"No, I need to know other things like how old is he? Is he tall? There are things a woman needs to know about the man she is going to wed and spend the rest of her days with."

"I know child but he gave us no time, none at all. I resisted as long as I could trying to arrange a visit but he would not hear of it. I ask you to be strong and do this for your land and King."

"What does he fear that time would reveal?"

"I do not know. The contracts are signed and that is the end of it. Either flee the country or wed."

"Please excuse me as I have things to attend and I flee from no man."

In the world of men there is no sympathy or regard for the lives of women thought Amanda. Their world consists of sword and shield and the sacrifice they make in battle that one moment where they live or die for king and country. The world of women consists of decades of sacrifice surrendered for daily obligations which seem trivial to men. Strong will and endurance is essential through years of toil for the ones they have a responsibility to provide and protect.

Amanda would do what was required of her as born to a position of power she had obligations to king and those that served. She would go to Brand Huxley and find peace with that man if not love. If he had a heart at all, she would search for ways to please and out of that would spring new life; if not out of love then from her dedication to those she served.

Amanda left her father's council disappointed with life and

with the man himself. She was only eighteen years old but had worked at being self-sufficient after the death of her mother two years ago. She wanted to show her father she could tend to business needing no one to find her way. He was of another world, the world of barter and trade. She was to be just another piece on his chessboard, a pawn to play at the right moment. Or maybe she was being too harsh; maybe her father was but a pawn on someone else's board. She would however go to Kara Keep and serve a master of his choosing. So was the life of the so called chosen, the life of the privileged.

Clorisa stood in the hall waiting.

"Well, tell me what is it?"

"I am to wed a man I have never met. I have been traded in exchange for peace in the north or some such nonsense."

"Refuse to go. Return to Mervin and stay there."

"No, I cannot do that. The King is involved. He would have my head for treason if I refused."

"What does the King have to do with your marriage?"

"Oh dear Clorisa. Mother tried to prepare me for this. She told me to find someone quickly before they found a man for me. I should have listened but I thought I was exempt. I have been looking after Mervin and the farms in my estate. I am self sufficient and pay tremendous amounts of taxes to the King but he wants more.

"I am to turn the northern frontier into a profitable land for him and make babies in my spare time. Next he will want me to take up a sword and become a knight as well."

"What do we do?"

"Go north Clorisa. We go north, like it or not."

Clorisa waited until Amanda retired that evening then

entered the duke's drawing room. This was not presumptuous on her part; she'd been in and out often on family business.

"What's going on?"

"In regards to what?" asked the Duke.

"Oh come now. Your daughter's marriage, what else?"

"It is not of your concern."

"I promised Judith on her death bed that I would care for Amanda and so I shall. So yes it is my affair, Winfred."

"And you have been given a tidy sum by Judith to do just that," said Winfred.

"The money has nothing to do with it and you know it."

"No I do not, so pray tell."

"Judith knew you would auction her off putting her money and lands into the hands of someone else. She gave me a tidy sum, as you put it, to care for her should some man leave her penniless. What have you done for her future, as a father, as a man?"

"So I am the villain in all of this and you the guardian angel."

"It looks that way, doesn't it."

"The king told me he was in dire straits and would have to double my levy unless…"

"Unless your daughter did his bidding and went north to marry Huxley," said Clorisa with disdain.

"Yes. He said it would relieve the burden on him."

"You sold her. Sold your daughter."

"Do you know what double the levy would mean? I would have to cut workers and drive the ones I had until they dropped. Everyone would suffer."

"Especially you, Lord."

"Everyone Clorisa, everyone. It is all up to her. My daughter, my love."

"Well, it's done and that's that."

Clorisa left the duke's study venomously in disgust of a man she'd admired until today. His daughter was little more than a token of negotiation to him. Judith his wife had seen through the man and saw this coming. She'd given her a great deal of gold deposited into her name in a Norman Bank across the channel where no one but she could claim it.

Signal fires burned from north to south then north again; soldiers knew the code. Her honour guard was on the way and would arrive in five days. Amanda rummaged through her closets filled with dresses, shoes, cloaks and a hundred other garments choosing the ones she would think to catch the eye of a lonely man in the northern world. Why else would he be in such haste? He would be surrounded by women dressed in burlap and lacking the grace for polite and interesting conversation. She would strive to be not only his lover but also his best friend, such were her goals.

Amanda met her honour guard on the front steps of Dorville, her father having other business to attend. There were twelve in all wearing the crest of Huxley; a bear bold and threatening. The captain dismounted and walked her way.

To say they were shabbily dressed would be a gross understatement. She looked at all the men searching for a garment that wasn't worn or frayed but found none. As a matter of fact not one garment was whole as they were all torn in one place or another. Her father would never let men out of the barracks looking like them.

Amanda had not seen her father more than a few days all of her life. She owed her birth to him only. All that she'd become was thanks to her mother not him. And now that she'd finally found peace and purpose after the tragedy of her mother's death he was sending her to a northern post to marry a stranger.

With these men.

"Good day Captain. Please ask your men to dismount so that we may dine before departing," said Amanda.

"We have orders to take you directly to the keep," said the captain.

"As you wish. My maid and I will be ready shortly."

There was no reason for such haste that Amanda could think of but rather than get into an argument about a meal she gave in. She didn't want to. She had given him an order and he disobeyed but then he was not officially hers to command at this time; not yet.

The stable hand gave here the reins to Sapphire: her Arab mare, part of her inheritance, it had been her mother's favourite horse. Amanda had given Clorisa one of her father's choice mounts, his most cherished. She did that little thing out of spite knowing his love for that horse. He'd said she was quick of whit and she wouldn't let him forget it. Amanda hoped he would not notice until they were long gone but if he did so what, it was the price he would have to pay, only a fraction of what he had made her surrender.

The packhorses containing her baggage were led to the soldiers.

The captain protested, "We have all the pack animals we need for this trip. We won't take two more."

"Take the horses captain or we will stay and you will ride back alone," said Amanda with an icy voice.

She looked into his eyes and he lowered his gaze not

uttering a sound. Deep inside she wanted him to continue her objections so she could call off the trip but the man backed down.

"The fool thinks he's in charge," said Clorisa.

Amanda was not about to ride a week in the same clothes and she would make him regret even trying to deprive her. Amanda had done something else with that little outburst; let him know who was in charge. The army was at her beckon and call, not the other way around. She'd had control of five hundred soldiers in two castles until today; now only twelve men answered her call but answer they would. Her dowry would pay for thousands of his kind.

CHAPTER 11

It was late in the year, the leaves starting to turn yellow and red. The bright sun did little to warm as a cold wind chilled the air especially at night. They were only a day north of Dorville and still riding through her lands. Amanda looked upon the estates feeling love in her heart and regret as it was probably the last time she would see her farms. Having grown and schooled here she was known by most and when met by someone on the road or nearby farm was warmly greeted. She could be recognized by her pure white horse from afar as few horses were as white as Sapphire.

As the sun set, the captain was riding past a road leading to a village not far away.

"Captain," yelled Amanda.

He pretended not to hear and rode forward not even acknowledging her call.

"Come with me Clorisa, we will stay at the inn. These fools can do whatever they want."

As she turned and rode toward the village the captain caught her and grasped the reins of her horse pulling it to a stop.

"My orders are to take you directly to the keep. This detour will cost us half a day."

Amanda reached within trying to find something in her

schooling that would have prepared her to deal with something like this but found nothing. She would try her best to handle the affair with dignity and grace, the way her mother would have. She was a lady and above crude language used in the world of men like him. Yet as soon as she opened her mouth all failed her.

Before she could put words together rage consumed her and not a sound sprung from her open mouth. Her right hand swung her whip catching the captain in the face. She pushed Sapphire forward into his horse feverishly swinging her whip at his face. He finally backed away, his horse stumbling almost sending him to the ground as Sapphire lunged forward in answer to his retreat.

Some of his men laughed but two came her way, a sinister look in their eyes. Clorisa rode between her and the soldiers.

"So what are you two brave men going to do now? Pull out your swords and slay two unarmed women? You make me sick," said Clorisa in a vile tone.

Amanda knew Clorisa would never let them pass while she still drew breath. That thought chilled her knowing that this would have to end. Her temper subsided and she was able to speak.

"You men attend me and not the other way around. One more incident like this and Clorisa and I will go home."

The captain came forward, staring into her eyes, a scowl on his face. He looked at her as though trying to make a decision, and then nodded.

"And Captain, if you ever touch my horse again then kill me instead because if you do not I will have you hung," said Amanda.

"I was only following orders."

"Until we reach the keep it is my orders you will follow. Do you think me to be a flower to be tended? We will go to the inn and not only spend the night but a whole day and another night. This will be the last time I see my lands. In another day we will be clear of them; they are still my lands."

The captain led the way to the village, a scowl on his face, and slight smiles from his men except two.

Clorisa wearing a wide grin said, "Why were you so easy on him?"

"I think I overreacted actually. My temper got the better of me. It could have been handled in a more ladylike way."

"These are not men of your world Amanda. They are a different breed. They understand action, not words. You stood your ground. It was either that or go along with them."

Amanda knew Clorisa was right, her servant was born in the north and would know men such as these; she did not.

Amanda and Clorisa were greeted at the inn run by a man she had played with as a child, Gibbin was his name. Gibbin's father had passed not long ago and he tended bar in place of his ailing mother. Gibbin was startled by a guard's approach as he sat at the table beside Amanda. She held up her hand in warning to the soldier not breaking the kind stare she was giving her old friend. Gibbin was such a warm lovable man and had a canny sense of humour; the kind of person she wanted to share her life with.

"Where are you going with this northern guard?" said Gibbin.

"Why north of course silly," taunted Amanda.

"You're leaving your lands?"

"Yes. I am to wed Duke Huxley within the week."

"I hadn't heard. It must have been sudden. Does he have you with child?"

"No silly, I have not even seen the man," said Amanda.

She choked on the last words and her mood turned serious.

"Another one of your father's bargains I'll wager," said Gibbin.

"Have you heard anything about the duke? I know nothing not even his age. Mary Bergen was matched to a nobleman seventy-one last year. Did you hear?"

"Yes but he died within six months leaving her most of his estate. They say he died in the bedroom. Mary wasn't a fool; she knew how to use what she had. As for the duke, men have passed with rumours, just rumours mind you."

"About what? Tell me."

"They say he is a hard man, a warrior and hunter. He keeps the northern tribes at bay. You'll not kill him in the bedroom from what I hear."

"Do not be silly, why would I want to kill him? You are the same as my father Gibbin. I want to know the things a woman wants to hear about a man."

"I know but those things I'm reluctant to speak of," said Gibbin and took her hand in his.

A soldier moved toward him and Amanda raised her head wearing a look that made him back away.

"I am sorry; these are not my soldiers, their Huxley's. Tell me dear friend. Would you not warn me if a snake was about to strike?"

"All right. He's rumoured to be a womanizer, has many a bastard child, takes what he wants. Now just rumours mind you," said Gibbin, a look of concern on his brow.

"Well he can not be too old if he is a womanizer, can he?"

"I don't know his age. I do know one other thing though. Tamus a trader from the north blames him for much of the unrest there. Says he is the cause for most of it. Again just the word of one man," said Gibbin showing more concern by the minute.

Amanda saw the worry upon his face and stroked his cheek, "Do not fret over me Gibbin. I can take care of myself."

"Oh, I know that. You used to out wrestle me. The other boys were afraid of you. I never did tell you that but it's true."

Amanda and Gibbin spent the evening talking of old times and old friends. She retired and the next day visited some of the people they had talked about. The day passed too quickly as did the night. The morning too soon in coming found them leaving the village far behind.

Amanda thought about Gibbin and others at the hamlet then suddenly realized something was causing her unrest. She looked about at the captain and his ten men.

Ten. The two who were definitely the Captain's friends were not there.

She turned Sapphire back to the village at a dead run, a thought had suddenly come to mind, one she dared not think about unless it could be proven true. The captain and two men followed but she knew had no chance of catching her on the plough horses they straddled.

Amanda galloped straight to the inn, leaping off her mount upon arrival. She rushed inside and saw two soldiers beating Gibbin. Amanda grabbed a pitcher setting on a table as she rushed by and struck an attacker over the head. He dropped as she wrestled with the other while Gibbin pulled the soldier's dagger from its sheath. The soldier's eyes went wide as Gibbin thrust the weapon into his stomach.

Amanda hugged her friend and said, "Oh, I am sorry to have brought this upon you."

Gibbin smiled and said, "I told you I wouldn't worry about you. You just proved that beyond doubt."

"Come, let us get you up and take a look at you."

Amanda helped her friend into a chair and removed his shirt as the captain and his men came in swords drawn.

"Put your swords away captain, two of your cowards beat my friend."

"They did it on their own. I gave no order," said the captain.

"And you did not notice them gone. No one told you two had deserted?" said Amanda in disgust.

"As I said they acted on their own and will be dealt with at the keep."

"This one won't be he's dead," said one of the soldiers.

"Who killed him? Not the barkeep?" said the captain.

"It was either that or get beat to death," said Gibbin.

Amanda saw a scowl form on the captain's face as he surveyed the scene. He looked in the back rooms for another but at this time of day would find only Gibbin's mother.

The other attacker struggled to his feet holding his head.

"Why did you beat my friend?" asked Amanda of the attacker.

"He shouldn't have touched you," said the man.

"Were you ordered to beat him?" asked Amanda.

The soldier looked at the captain then back to her, "No it was our own doing."

After tending to Gibbin Amanda reluctantly mounted Sapphire and started her way north again. She knew the captain had given the order to beat and maybe even kill Gibbin. That kind of jealousy was normally shown only by a lover or someone possessive unless he himself had orders to regard her as property, the duke's possession. Maybe it was a standing order among them to regard his women in that manner; kill anyone who even touches them. What was she riding into?

Amanda thought about turning back, telling the story to her father and ask he reconsider. No, was her next thought for two reasons: he would just tell her to go again and secondly, she did not think the captain would let her turn around. And that was the thought that sent a chill through her, she was a prisoner.

"Clorisa. Do you think we should turn around and go back?"

"It's up to you. I don't think they have any intentions of hurting us. If they wanted to they could have already done so. I think that they have a crude sense of right and wrong. Violence is the way with men of the north. You have to get used to that Mandy. Stand your ground the way you've been doing. I'll stand by you."

Clorisa always called her Mandy when consoling her, always did. It made her feel at ease.

Amanda thought about running; her horse and the one Clorisa rode were too fast to be caught by their escort. Where to though and for what purpose; she still had a duty to King and country. And what was she running from? For all she knew the duke could be a warm kind man, showering her with love and devotion for many years to come. Amanda would not judge the man by a rogue captain he had in his service. She had had some difficulties with an officer in her father's troops and knew the trouble they could cause. She would have him dealt with at the keep.

Once they arrived. If they did.

By the time she arrived at the keep the winter storms may have already begun. It was a strange time for a wedding. They could have waited until spring, given her time to think and grow into her future.

Their escort appeared to be in a foul mood most of the time. Today they rode under fair skies, the sun shinning. It was cold but not frigid, a gentle breeze. They rode on a carpet of lively colours, gold and red. It was a glorious day bringing music to her heart. Their escort rode as though in a swamp during a rain storm. No love of life in their hearts.

They had exchanged no more than a dozen words with these men in all this time, all words in discord.

CHAPTER III

The chipmunk hid in the rotted trunk of an old oak that had not yet fallen. Winter was coming and he'd not enough food stored to last him through that icy season. The squirrels had bullied their way and retrieved the fattest acorns and other nuts. They were not inclined to share. He'd been quick though and got a few for himself but not enough.

He was about to descend and rummage through the leaves for whatever those red bushy tailed devils had left behind. He heard something rustling through the leaves. It could be a herd of wild boar. His heart thumped out of control. He wanted to scream but forced himself to be silent. He crouched low and from the shadows stared in the direction of the sound.

They were humans riding their beasts, he'd seen them before. There were over ten all dressed alike and two more that were not. They were stopping and climbing from their beasts to the ground. Had they seen him? Did they know where he was? His heart thumped. He was too frightened to run.

They didn't walk his way, only kicked leaves aside and stacked dead branches in a pile. Then they made it burn the way lightning in the summer started trees on fire. They brought out big grey globes and hung them over the fire. The two that were different sat on a log and watched. A little house of cloth was being built, a lot smaller than the ones in the village down the road.

The chipmunk watched as they ate, his stomach growling and his mouth watering at the sight. Oh look at that, they were dropping food. He watched in apprehension. Were they picking it up? No, they let it lie. He looked toward the sun almost touching the ground. Soon it would be dark.

He was afraid to go out at night; the world was full of hidden evil waiting in the dark. But maybe, just maybe, at twilight he could go and take a look. The two that were different climbed into the little house as the men sat around the fire and drank from leather skins. He shivered not wanting to become an article of clothing or a drinking flask. They were noisy, the nosiest people he'd ever seen. It was his chance though to see what they'd left on the ground. He scurried through the leaves, the noise hidden by the racket they made. These people were easy prey.

He found bread, he loved bread and there was more. He looked up suddenly. Was it a trap? No, they were busy talking around the fire. He gathered what ever he could find and hid it in his tree. Darkness set in as he slept peacefully beside his booty. They would remember the day they'd messed with him.

The chipmunk was awakened by the noise at dawn. Had they discovered the missing food? Were they outraged and looking for him? No. They ate more food then gathered their possessions and left. He picked up more bread and an apple core. What a feast. He hoped more of their kind would drop by and visit.

The relentless noise was starting to get on Amanda's nerves.

The clatter of weapons and rustling of leaves as horses trudged their way hock deep through the scarlet and yellow drifts. The cold especially in the evenings and at dawn was also wearing her down. In the evenings the captain and his men sat around the only campfire. To join him she would have to force her way in and sit amongst the rabble in scorn. In little ways like this, building only one fire, the captain was exacting revenge on her for putting him in his place. She would do it again though, even if she had to freeze. You couldn't let the hired help rule, her father used to say. The captain was being paid to protect and not enslave.

Clorisa hugged her and said, "Tomorrow I'll build a fire for us Mandy. It's too late today. Almost dark, too dark to find dry wood."

"Can you do that?"

"Sure. I was on my own before your mother accepted me into servitude."

"That soldier, the one with the jet black hair, he keeps looking at you," said Amanda.

"I've noticed and also where he stares, not in my eyes."

"Oh, here he comes. He must have sensed we were talking about him," said Amada.

The soldier walked toward Clorisa, a wry smile on his handsome face.

"Why don't we go for a little evening stroll, Clorisa. That's your name isn't it. My name's Chad."

"If I walked into the bush with you I wouldn't be much of a lady would I? What are you insinuating Chad? After all my virtue is in question here?" said Clorisa.

Chad stood dumfounded with a look of confusion on his face.

Amanda shook her head then said, "I think you put that a little too eloquently Clorisa. Remember what you told me of men from the north? Chad listen. What Clorisa is trying to say is that by merely asking her to walk into the woods with you, especially in front of the others, you are calling her a tramp."

Chad looked at his feet then smiled and said, "We can wait for the others to fall asleep."

It was Clorisa's turn to shake her head, "Go away Chad."

Amanda glanced at Clorisa and smiled to herself. At twice her age her maid drew men like no other she had ever seen. Clorisa was a beautiful woman yet showed no interest in men. And maybe that was part of her charm. They wanted what they couldn't have. Amanda at half Clorisa's age wished she was half as pretty as her maid.

That night was spent by Amanda and Clorisa in the cold while the men sat around a campfire. There were no inns here, they would find few towns large enough to support travellers this far north. The soldiers had pitched a crude tent barely large enough for her and Clorisa. They slept on cold ground huddled together for warmth, Clorisa wrapping her arms around her as she had done when young. They were like sisters, Amanda sharing all with her maid; told her everything, even her most intimate thoughts. One thing she could not tell Clorisa was the extent of her fear and anxiety over the duke; the man terrified her.

"What do you think of this duke Clorisa?"

"I think him to be a leader of men you are unfamiliar with. The enlisted soldiers in the lands to the north are mercenaries and men on the run. Many are thieves and murderers fleeing the hangman from crimes committed here in the south or other lands.

"It is a land where you don't ask a man's past. You take him for what he is. If he can use a sword then you hire him, no questions asked. You pay him knowing if you did not he would be gone the next day. They are people and a land I hoped you could avoid. They are soldiers and keepers of the so called peace in the north."

Amanda choked on those words.

"Another words, I am heading into the lands of heathen tribes?"

"Simply put. Yes."

Her mother had told Amanda Clorisa had come from the north seeking work in a better land. She felt badly dragging her maid and friend back to where she'd come from.

"I'm sorry you are part of this. I never meant to get you involved. You can turn back if you want. I'll give you a letter that will gain you employment anywhere you choose."

"Silly Mandy. Where you go, so do I."

Amanda hugged Clorisa and fell asleep in her arms the way she had her whole life.

Amanda washed her face in stream as the soldiers packed the tent and blankets. Clorisa combed the tangles out of her hair as they waited for their escort to ready.

Amanda mounted Sapphire and rode between the soldiers, six ahead and five behind, Clorisa as usual by her side. She thought about the Gibbin's rumours; about many females and of bastard children. Her father had been accused of such things by women hoping for money in trade for silence. All men of money and power were preyed upon in many ways. Amanda's mother had once told her that the tales of her father were rubbish and knew they could not be true. As for the trader and his statements about the duke being responsible for most of the trouble in the north; well maybe he had spent a few days in one of the duke's jails. Gossip is cheap and the truth is usually so well guarded that no one would ever know.

Amanda was back where she started. Having discarded the rumours was again left with nothing; knew nothing of the man she would spend the rest of her life with other than he was in a hurry to meet her.

The flat farming lands of her country were giving way to hills, steeper and higher as time passed. Farms and cottages were few and far between as the road turned into a trail, not wide enough to ride side by side in places. Amanda would have to look over her shoulder when talking to Clorisa which caused her discomfort but talk she must as there was nothing else to do.

This far north the leaves on the trees were already falling laying a blanket of red and gold over the cold ground. The winds bit deep especially when cresting a hill and after the sun abandoned them. The captain pointed to the ruins of trading settlement which he said was the halfway point in their journey. She was halfway there, half way to her new life.

Every season had its own smell. The clean crisp odour of winter, the sharp fresh smell of spring, the fragrance of summer flowers, and now the acidy, pungent scent of dead leaves; the death of another year. Amanda fought depression at the lowest point in her short life. She was riding away from her home, in the cold, with a group of men who probably despised her. She was freezing, felt hungry, and dirty. More than anything she needed a hot bath. She smelled of dead leaves, horse, and smoke.

Soon she would be at the keep in a warm bed though.

Yet not alone.

Amanda panicked at that thought. She'd never had to think about that before until now; dream yes, there were dreams but dreams were sweeter than reality. Reality was frightening. She would not be in bed alone.

"A penny for your thoughts," said Clorisa.

"They would be childish thoughts. I am a woman and have to live up to certain expectations. I have a role to fulfil both for man and nature. I cannot always have things my own way."

"Don't take things so serious. We'll make it all work out somehow," said Clorisa.

It was a cold windy day bare branches reaching for the sky; whirlwinds of red and gold leaves formed ghosts all around. The sun was faint in the iron sky, the threat of a storm loomed on the horizon.

Lightning cracked and thunder rolled as Amanda and Clorisa huddled in their tent finding it impossible to stay dry. The wind blew through the open front and lifted the sides. Out of frustration they pulled the tent down upon themselves using it as a waterproof blanket instead.

No cooking was done that evening leaving only wet bread for their evening meal.

The morning brought no relief as they rode in wind and rain. The day wore on and seemed never to end when they came upon a farm, a large barn not far from the stone cottage. The captain knocked upon the door and was soon greeted by a big man. He shook the captain's hand and pointed to big structure not far in the distance.

The soldiers put the horses in a corral and all sat within the out building. Not long afterwards two hooded figures appeared with food held before them. One of them put a pot on a stool and pulled down her hood revealing a middle aged woman, a warm smile on her face. The other hooded figure carried a sack and handed pieces of bread to everyone. She pulled down her hood and took off the thick garment causing the men, each and everyone to swallow as their eyes went wide.

Standing before them was a young blonde woman wearing a revealing burlap dress. Her hips and breasts were more than ample, her waist small and tight. Her smile and moves taunted them, she was young and naïve.

Amanda took one look at the soldiers and knew trouble was coming to the young lady like it or not. One of them was already heading her way cheap compliments spilling from his mouth. The older woman eyed the soldiers and knew they were not here to protect. She looked closer as her mouth opened wide.

"Are you or are you not from Barkley Castle?" asked the woman.

Amanda knew that Barkley was the farthest northern outpost in her father's lands, probably a day southwest.

"We're from Kara Keep," said one of the soldiers.

Those words made the woman tremble as she grasped her daughter and both rushed back to the cottage. The men ate quickly looking at each other as though speaking in some noiseless tongue. A silent agreement had been made and they all rose to their feet as if of one mind. Amanda watched the captain as he smiled, nodding in consent to those unspoken words.

Amanda knew that harsh words would not stop these men,

they would simply ignore her. She had already seen they had no sense of fair play and justice was not a part of their lives. Their attack on Gibbin proved that. Amanda had pledged to protect people such as these and would do what she could. The family had offered hospitality and kindness toward the soldiers and now must suffer for their good deeds.

"What do we do Clorisa?"

"Let's run to the house and get them out of here before it starts."

Amanda ran ahead of the men toward the house with Clorisa at her heels. She pounded on the door and pushed it open as the big man and a younger son rose to their feet from the dinner table. Amanda and Clorisa pushed the women out of a back door but were stopped by two soldiers already there. They took the blonde haired girl and pulled her screaming toward the barn. From outside of the cottage Amanda heard grunts as the two men inside were overrun. The older woman ran screaming into the woods toward a well worn path revealed by lightning strikes as she sprinted to a destination known only to her.

Amanda looked inside the cottage and found the beaten men. They were hurt, unable to stand due to the wounds they had received. She and Clorisa tended the men cleaning wounds and tying bandages around the bleeding gashes.

Amanda stood at the cottage door feeling helpless knowing there was nothing she could do for the young girl. She would have to wait until the soldiers had finished and salvage whatever was left. Tears of pity ran from her eyes mingled with raindrops. Eleven men would have her this night with no more regard than if they were butchering a cow. She could only wonder what would remain after this single night; the young girl just wanting to flirt with the boys.

Time went by then after seeing no movement inside Amanda and Clorisa entered the barn. Men were asleep everywhere and in the middle of the barn laying upon the floor was the girl. Her eyes glared into nothingness, her body limp, looking lifeless. There was blood and bruises upon her breasts and lower body. Amanda and Clorisa carried her into the cottage and tended to her as best they could. The girl did not utter a sound and probably didn't even know they were there.

Amanda and Clorisa spent the rest of the night trying to aid the young woman and the two men. By morning the young woman was asleep, her eyes finally closed. Her father was up on his feet unable to speak as he regarded the damage around him.

Amanda walked out of the front door and watched as the older woman came home from wherever she had run the night before. Amanda lost count as forty or so men carrying all manner of weapons descended upon the farm. The woman walked into the cottage and soon returned.

"You two leave this place. You helped me and I thank you for that. May the Gods bless you. Now go quickly we have work to do," said the woman.

Amanda and Clorisa mounted their horses as the soldiers looked on, swords drawn. Clorisa took the packhorse with supplies leading it from the yard behind her own. Amanda left the other two pack horses with her personal items to the woman and her daughter. The soldier's expressions were blank knowing they would never leave this place alive. Who could have guessed there was a village nearby? They had brought it on themselves thought Amanda. They rode from the farm as the sound of clanging metal and tortured men filled the air behind them.

It was a law of humanity that the strong look after the weak, the old tend to the young and the healthy nurse the sick. These men felt no compulsion to respect the basic rules of man. They were self indulgent animals, no more than that. Their death was not revenge but necessity.

CHAPTER IV

Amanda and Clorisa were alone and lost, riding in a direction they believed to be north. Amanda searched for ways to secure the direction they were taking but was never quite sure of the path she chose. The sun rose in the east, moved south, and then set in the west or so they said. North must be opposite the sun at midday but the trail in front of her moved east and west. Moss grew on the north side of a tree she was told. After kicking leaves from the base of twenty trees she finally found some moss but it grew half way around. So which way was north? Amanda stayed on the widest paths she could find.

"Which way Clorisa?"

"I don't know. I'm not familiar with this part of the country. It's not where I was born."

It was not a matter of food for them as the pack horse was loaded with enough for over ten people, or water as there were many streams. It was the cold nights they had to escape and growing colder with the passing days.

"Oh no," said Clorisa.

"What?"

"I've seen that grove of trees before and look, look our horses' hoof prints."

"We're going around in circles, we'll have to pick a

landmark and ride toward it. Follow the trail narrow or wide that takes us in that direction," said Amanda.

"Which landmark?"

"Well, the sun's high in the sky as it's going to be so we'll say that's south. Look at those hills opposite the sun and see that break between the highest ones. We'll head for that break."

"So be it. We have to go toward something; it might as well be that."

Amanda was not sure if they should abandon the journey north and try to find their way south instead. If they did that they would have to find their way in that direction as well. They were over half way to Kara Keep so would ride north for another day and decide. If they aborted the journey they would have to wait for another escort and repeat the process so turning back would be a last resort.

They camped under an open sky as the tent was too clumsy for them to pitch. They huddled together beside the warm fire and talked of days gone by and loved ones lost. At thirty-six Clorisa was eighteen years senior to Amanda but was considered a friend equalled by none. Amanda shared her duties with the maid even entrusting use of her personal seal on vital documents. They both had the key to the castle's treasury at Dorville.

"I've never asked this and maybe it's not my place but have you ever been in love Clorisa?"

"Oh yes, so I have. With a young knight, His armour and smile like gleaming gold."

"So what happened?"

"He died in some senseless display of pride. He was challenged by another who cheated him of life, a despicable ruse. The other was sentenced to death for his treacherous act. But my love, my life was gone before my eyes. He was forever lost."

That story sent a chill through Amanda.

"Why did you never tell me of this before?"

"I could never speak of it until now, especially since you're in a worse situation than I was."

"We're the victims of men, aren't we?"

"In a way. We're attached to the good and evil they do. We're bound to them through wedlock and the laws of man."

Amanda had a lot to think about on this northern road to the rest of her life, if she could find the way, if she could live through it all.

The hooting of owls and the howl of wolves sounded through the night. It was the sound of predators stalking unwary and unprotected prey.

The next morning found them packed and underway before the sun fully showed itself under the cloudless sky. Travelling was slow as they moved from one trail to the next keeping that far mountain gap in sight. Water in a stream they crossed hurriedly flowed over and between rocks letting nothing stand in its way as it rushed through the land to the sea. A frightened dear bounded through the woods as the roar of a predator sounded in frustration for letting it escape.

Halfway through the day as they stopped to water their horses, the snapping of an axe breaking the sound of the woods called to them.

They followed the sound and came upon an old man splitting wood in front of his stone and thatched cottage. They watched for a time and after seeing no one else decided to approach and ask for help. Upon their arrival the man wiped his brow and leaned on his axe.

"Good day ladies, I'm Jarrid, can I be of help?"

"Good day sir, I'm Amanda and this is Clorisa. We're trying to locate Kara Keep. Can you help us?" asked Amanda.

"I can but why would you want to go there?"

"It's going to be our new home," said Amanda.

"It's not the place for two young ladies dressed in finery and riding mounts such as yours."

"Well.. It's a long story," said Amanda too embarrassed to tell all.

"All right come on down, we'll have something to drink and I'll tell you how to get there."

They dismounted and put their horses in a pen then followed the man into his home. He made three cups of herb tea that Amanda was familiar with; it was tangy and settled the nerves. The old man sat with a sigh and leaned back in his chair.

"I've been to Kara Keep a few times over the years. It's a tough place full of soldiers and mercenaries. It's the northern most defence against tribes that live north of the keep."

"Has anyone ever tried to make peace with these people?" asked Amanda.

"Not to my knowledge, but then to tell the truth I don't really know."

"They're just people like everyone else. They don't want to loose their children to war any more than I would," said Amanda.

"I know a trader named Tarus that knows a chief of those tribes, Rogun. From what he tells me and from what I've seen with my own eyes I believe it's all about gold paid to the duke by the King. No fighting, no gold. So I believe it's in the best interest of the duke that the fighting goes on. Now that's just my opinion, the word of an old man."

"It's worth as much to me as the word of anyone else. Do you live here alone?" said Amanda.

"Well, since my wife Mary died and my three sons ran off to join that army of the duke's."

"I'm sorry about your wife," said Clorisa.

"Oh, that's all right it's been three winters now that she's passed."

"And how do we get to the keep?" asked Amanda.

"Just set your sights on the cleft between the two biggest peaks to the north and Kara Keep is dead centre."

"That's the way we were headed."

"It's late afternoon so why not stay for supper and then the night. In the morning I'll take you to a road which will save you a lot of time."

"As long as it's no trouble."

"It would be the best time I've had since, well since before my Mary passed."

"Thank you, yes, we'll accept your offer gladly," said Amanda.

They ate a feast that evening, pork, potatoes, vegetables, and drank excellent homemade wine. They slept in a warm stone cottage near the hearth, reluctant to rise for a morning meal already waiting. After more chatter and some laughter they saddled their horses and followed Jarrid to a road that would take them to the keep. They thanked their host for his kindness and waved good bye.

Amanda had a lot on her mind as she followed the road leading to the twin peaks. She thought about her escort, the captain and his rogue soldiers. What they had done to her friend Gibbin and the kind folk at the farm. Like mad dogs they had taken that young girl with no more regard to her than a prostitute, maybe less. Hopefully their lives ended without to much blood lost by their executioners, the villagers who sought justice for wrongs dealt to their friends. Amanda would never forget the look upon the farmer's wife when she learned they were from Kara Keep. It was as though she was looking at demons from the dark place.

Jarrid's words were of further concern to her. The old gentle woodsman had no good thoughts of the keep and had more concern for the heathens that they fought.

Without warning soldiers rode from the woods beside the trail and surrounded them, their horses unable to move leaving no way to run. They were not wearing the Huxley crest and were certainly forward and frightening in their ways. Maybe they meant to be.

"What is the meaning of this?" asked Amanda.

"You're on Cabot land. State your business," said the captain.

"We're on our way to Kara Keep so please let us pass," said Amanda.

"You're a long way west for that," said the captain.

"Well, please direct us then and we will be on our way."

"I think you'd better come with us my lady and see Lord Cabot. I have a feeling he'll want to meet you," said the captain.

They rode with an escort in a direction toward the setting sun; west when Amanda wanted to go north. She didn't have any choice in the matter as their armed guards gave them no room to run. They were prisoners again; first Huxley's men and now Cabot's lot, whoever Lord Cabot was. Were all the men of the north so violent towards others; what kind of a land was she heading to.

It was already dark when Amanda saw torches glowing in the distance. As they came closer a castle formed in the dim light emitted from the walls. On command the gates swung open when they arrived, soldiers on the ramparts staring their way as though never having seen women before. They were directed to a keep inside the castle walls and entered, the light as dim inside as in the castle yard.

Few torches burned along the inner walls as they were directed toward a dining area where a single man sat at the head of a table. He held a meaty bone in his hand, his beard soaked with fat, his fingers covered with grease as well. He raised his brow as they entered but kept chewing the bone; he seemed inquisitive in his look but ravenous as well. He stared at them, relentlessly gnawing at his bone then curiosity won over appetite. He wiped his beard and hands in a towel and threw it on the table before him as though angry over the intrusion.

"And who would you be?" he rasped then finally stood and walked their way.

Like his soldiers he was acting in a threatening manner when none existed. They were only two women and definitely not highwaymen, no threat to a castle full of soldiers. Amanda looked him up and down trying to be slightly intimidating in return. It wasn't much but all she had; women had to do these little things to hold their own.

"My name is Amanda Daggot and this is my maid Clorisa. I am on my way to see Duke Huxley at Kara Keep. Your soldiers stopped us and brought us here against our will. I ask you let us continue our journey."

"Well, I see, now what would your business be with him?"

"It is personal and not your affair."

"You're in my castle now and on my land. I make it my affair so tell me what I ask," Cabot yelled.

"I suppose it is no secret that the Duke and I are to wed," said Amanda.

She didn't want to give in to the man, not even a little, but he was being more threatening than ever so she did not want to take any chances.

"Hah, and you ride alone with no guard."

"Our guards were killed by villagers two days south."

"Why?"

"They raped a young woman."

"Hah. Sounds like Huxley's bunch, all criminals and thieves."

Amanda asked him more out of sarcasm then anything else, "You are not friends then?"

They expect me to be stupid so that is what I will give them she thought.

"Hah, a friend to that spineless bag of wind. If it wasn't for his knights I'd have killed the man years ago."

By the sound of his voice and the look in his eyes Amanda knew she was not in a good position here and thought she would soften her approach with this man. She and Clorisa could be killed or enslaved and none would be the wiser.

"I don't know the man myself. It was an arranged marriage by my father and the king. I have actually never even seen him and if I find you to be true then I will simply leave."

"You're not missing anything by not knowing him and are fortunate you've been spared his company so far."

"That may be but I feel I have an obligation to at least meet the man as I have promised the king."

"I've a blood oath to kill him if that helps you understand the matter," said Cabot.

"I am not him and ask you to remember I am here at the king's request."

"The king knows of our feud. He taxes me and gives the gold to Huxley for his so called defence of the north. I don't regard him as my king so owe him nothing."

Amanda knew that any further discussion would only infuriate the man so it would be wise to draw it to a conclusion.

"Are we to continue our journey or not? What is your final word?"

"You'll have a room here for the night and we'll talk in the morning after I sleep on it."

They were escorted upstairs through the dingy castle and given a room, a single candle for light. Food was brought to them and a guard stood at their door. The guard was what worried Amanda. What could two women do? Only run and he was afraid of that. Why?

"Our situation looks desperate," whispered Clorisa.

"Mother said that even the worst man has a conscience so I will play on that. I cannot let him think I am appeasing him though or he will harden. I will do it gently, it is all we have."

"I don't think anything you do will help Mandy. I think his hate for Huxley rules him. I think I'll have to kill the man," said Clorisa.

"How?"

"I have an herb in my bag that in proper amounts can heal or in a high dose can kill. If I go to my grave so does he."

The night was full of sounds as the wind howled almost as loud as the drunken soldiers in the courtyard below. Lord Cabot appeared to be yelling at someone and could be heard through the closed door. A woman screamed and he laughed as though it pleased him. Amanda had seen his bridled rage in the dining room. Cabot acted as though he was looking for a reason to unleash it; she'd not given him one.

Cabot had been sitting in the dining room himself, eating alone. That said a lot about the man and none of it was good. She had sensed from her father that the king had little control in the north and depended on Huxley to keep the peace. The Duke was draining his treasury yet he still paid and maybe men like Cabot was his reason for doing so. She had met no one so far that had anything good to say about her husband to be and now met a man with a blood oath to kill him.

Amanda's one regret was being born a woman in these times, as though she'd had a choice. When was God going to give women a chance to prove they could do better than men? There would be less slaughter and loss of life with women in control. Respect would be had for sons by not sending them to die in war. Their daughters would not be enslaved or raped. Amanda laughed to herself; she was such a dreamer, so be it.

Don't dreamers change the world sometimes? She'd always felt sorry for herself being born to serve a man; not able to live a life of her own choosing. Mother had always told her to do the best with whatever came her way. The tree at the crest of a mountain will never yield to the wind; a healthy rabbit will always outrun a fox. There was always hope for those who never gave up and none for those that do.

Except for the howling wind all was finally quiet. All those drunken men must have passed out. Amanda though worried and afraid found sleep.

Morning came to them with a crunch and a thud as the door burst open.

"Out of bed and downstairs," said the captain of the guard.

They were taken to the dining hall where Lord Cabot was already busy chewing on pork chops. Amanda ate little waiting for her host to finish so they could be informed of their fate. He looked to be in no hurry as Amanda glanced at him occasionally with a slight smile prodding for a response. Clorisa also ate sparingly and looked impatient waiting for the man to speak. Finally he patted his mouth with a towel and wiped his hands.

"You're both going to have a little accident east of here, far from these castle walls. I will not let Huxley benefit from anything if I can help it. I looked through your bags and found papers that state you go to him with a rather large dowry. I won't permit that. He takes enough from me already so in turn I take from him," said Cabot.

Amanda watched Clorisa as she walked toward the big man smiling, touching his shoulder, passing her hand over his cup, dropping something in. It was so subtle if she'd not looked for it then it would have been missed.

"We have more to offer than you could possibly imagine," said Clorisa.

"You offer trouble, nothing more. Be gone with you wench," said Cabot.

"We have nothing to do with your feud. I have hurt no one," said Amanda.

"I'll speak no further on this subject. Captain take them away," said Cabot. Then he took the cup and gulped down the contents.

Clorisa's mouth turned into a slight grin.

They were led to the courtyard, their horses already saddled and soldiers waiting. Amanda's pleading eyes scanned the courtyard for someone that would help. The few people within the castle walls turned their backs as though knowing her plight and giving answer to her silent request.

They rode through the morning no respect from the soldiers as they talked of rape before the killings to come. Amanda stayed silent feeling like a rabbit in the mouth of a wolf. How could they possibly escape this?

Half a day east of the castle soldiers came from the woods as before. This time the soldiers were wearing the Huxley crest. They pushed Cabot's men out of the way then surrounded Amanda and Clorisa. The man leading them was without question a knight and a gallant one at that.

"We'll take the ladies off your hands. We've been looking for them everywhere. Thank you for finding them," said the knight.

The knight then smiled at Cabot's captain with a look in his eyes that said, "Do something please." They were evenly matched both with six soldiers each at their backs.

Cabot's captain reached for his sword and the knight drew his before the other man's was half out. He would be dead now if the knight had wanted it so. Cabot's captain grinned and rode away with his men in tow.

Amanda was so impressed and relieved she was ready to giggle but held back.

"Thank you kind sir and may I ask your name?"

"Damon Roth, first knight to Duke Huxley at your service."

"They were going to kill us. Some sort of feud between Cabot and the Duke."

"Yes, I know. Their stable boy rode through the night and found our camp on the way to the keep. Oh tell no one of him as he works for us and keeps us informed. He told us of your plight."

"What will be done with Cabot?"

"Probably nothing, the threat will be reported to the king but as no harm has been done it will be ignored. Cabot is a source of much needed revenue. There is a delicate balance between the nobility in the north that the king would never upset. He needs men like Cabot in case Huxley turns on him. It's a hard thing to understand."

"For a woman you mean. I can assure you dear knight I know exactly of what you speak and have dealt with matters such as those myself," said Amanda, sorry that she snapped at him.

She had lunged at the man who had saved her life; that quick wit and loose tongue were going to make trouble for her as everyone had warned. She was upset to find that someone who had almost taken her and Clorisa's life was to go unpunished.

"I apologize for that. I speak before thinking at times," she said.

"No offence taken dear lady."

"You were looking for us then?" she said wanting to change the subject.

"No just out on patrol. I said that we were looking for you for their benefit only so they would look for no informants, they would find the boy as he was probably the only one who left that night. I didn't even know you were lost until the boy came to us."

Damon stared at Cabot's soldiers as they rode out of sight.

"Whatever happened to your guard? The duke sent twelve men."

"Killed by villagers after they raped a young girl and almost killed her parents."

"Sounds like some of his men. The ones he sent were mercenaries and worse than most of the rest."

"Why would he send them then?"

"They're better at their job than the enlisted."

Amanda felt relief wash over her as a great weight had been taken off her shoulders. It was the first time in days she'd felt truly safe. Amanda was so happy she felt giddy. She gazed upon the young knight's face and broke into a smile. His blonde hair and blue eyes gave him a warm friendly look, the kind of man people naturally warm to. When he returned her smile she knew that if he were the ambassador to her future at the keep she had a good life awaiting her.

"We will take you to Kara Keep in place of your other escort. Follow me if you please my lady."

"Yes kind sir."

Amanda looked at Clorisa and smiled, her maid in turn raising her brow and smiled as well. He was definitely an impressive man. It was not easy to make an impact on Clorisa, she'd been hurt by many a man in her youth. The young knight was exceptionally well mannered as he rode ahead and they followed directly behind him. He also did them the courtesy of staying far enough ahead so their conversations would be private. She was looking forward to her first glimpse of Kara Keep as the rumours and ill thoughts washed from her mind.

Clorisa spoke in a low voice, "As for Cabot, he will not last the day. He drank what was in his cup this morning. I put something in it that will help him to sleep, forever. I would not let him sentence us to death without suffering as well."

"I know I saw you. That was bold."

Amanda looked toward her maid not knowing what to think. She would kill Cabot without a second thought. That was what she did when she passed her hand over his cup before touching his shoulder and pleading for her life. Amanda was in deadly company, her maid servant and a knight. She felt safe.

CHAPTER V

The young knight told them that it was only two days journey to Kara Keep so they would stay overnight at a farm where he was welcome. Amanda felt that Damon would probably be welcome at a lot of farms especially the ones owned by fathers seeking a husband for one of their daughters. If he was the one she had been sent to marry disappointment would not cross her mind.

Knowing him for only a half day she felt he had a heart and soul a woman could work on. He would react to kindness and love forming an endless chain of emotions for both. But he was not to be the one, hers was still two days away and if half the gentleman of his first knight then she would be indeed delighted.

Clorisa tapped her arm and said, "I think you're smitten by that knight."

"He saved our lives, so yes I am a little taken aback by him."

"Remember he's a stranger Mandy," whispered Clorisa.

"I know. I know."

This day did not drag, filled with excitement and hope the time passed quickly. Sunset brought on the chill of the night, the kind that creeps into the bones but as luck would have it they would sleep near a hearth again.

The farmer welcomed the knight with open arms. He was an old man; he and his wife greeted them warmly. He was an old soldier giving up his sword for a plough before luck abandoned him. When Amanda entered the home she saw the trappings of a knight hanging on the wall above the mantel. She was immediately impressed and wondered why the drastic change to farm life.

"This is Kale and his wife Hayly, and this is Lady Daggot and Clorisa," said Damon.

"Good day to you both and thank you for your kindness," said Amanda.

"Please sit and we'll dine shortly," said Hayly.

"Could you find no other work at the castle other than fighting? I'm sorry I ask only as soldier to farmer is unusual," said Amanda.

"No at the keep it's either fight if fit or get out. There are enough men crippled from battle to do chores," said Kale.

"Have attempts at peace ever been made with the northern tribes?" asked Amanda.

"Tread lightly or not at all on that subject my lady, as the duke considers it no ones business but his own and I say that only because I am no longer at the keep," said Kale.

"You are entering the world of fighting men, different from your world in the south. I won my title east of you as a soldier for the King, a world like yours so know of what I speak," said Damon.

"You want me to listen and not speak. Is that what you suggest?" said Amanda.

"No my lady, please forgive me. I suggest only that you discover your new world before you attempt to change it as it may not be yours to change," said Damon.

"I see. Then the duke rules is that what you mean?" said Amanda.

"Yes in a way my lady," said Damon.

"Damon, I will chastise no one for speaking their mind and ask only you do so without malice. I will listen and repeat nothing," said Amanda.

"You are wise for your age my lady. The duke is a warrior and does things his way to whatever end of his choosing, he listens to no one," said Damon.

"And he will punish those who oppose him in any way. He may even see a suggestion as a threat, so take care my lady, take great care," said Kale.

"You make him out to be a monster," said Amanda.

"No, he's not that, just the kind of man you're not aware of. His life is with men and not women, you'll see what we speak of," said Damon.

Amanda ate supper disheartened again thinking about what the two knights had told her. She believed them both to be good men with kind hearts and knew their intent was not malicious. She had been given a warning to tread lightly and would take their advice as the words came from their hearts. Her husband to be was becoming more of a mystery day by day and her fear of him grew as well. He was not a monster but preferred the company of men? She wondered what that meant but would push the two no further for answers. At this point she actually wanted to hear no more of him and would wait; see for herself what he was all about. He was only a day away now.

Amanda slept little that night waking constantly ill at ease with her future. She wished to turn around, go home to her lands and live out her days as a spinster. Her inheritance was the curse that put her in this situation. Too much land, too much money made her a target for the first man the King had to appease. A dowry like hers was a King's ransom and she wished it had been scant instead, just a farm or two to manage and a horse to ride. A man like Gibbin for a husband, no one to worry over besides the children she would bear.

Amanda felt she had not been blessed with beauty and was in fact plain. She could however with colours and eye shades make herself somewhat appealing. She was thin and lacked the breasts and hips that men admired. Her long brown hair curled half way down her back and was probably her strongest asset. Her brown eyes and pale complexion would set no man aback. Gibbin had told her many times that her intelligence was what she should tout; told she had been blessed with that. Both knights had advised her against that though with the duke. Amanda would do as they suggested, go to the keep and stay quiet, act dumb. It was probably what a warrior wanted and expected.

Amanda wished she looked more like Clorisa. At thirty-six her maid had maintained an excellent figure, turning men's heads if she wore a tight dress. Her red hair and hazel eyes gave her a look that would not be missed. Her delicate features took ten years off her age.

Morning finally came after a night of no sleep. This day she would meet her husband to be. Her excitement had waned and she just wanted to get it over with. Since a mere girl of seven she had always pictured her wedding day as one filled with cheer and love. Amanda saw the castle full of smiling faces and women crying. She saw her handsome husband dressed as a king and her father at her side. Amanda saw carriages drawn by white horses and flowers filling the air as they descended on her and her love. She heard bells chime and people cheer, not once did she dream of any less.

And now she just wanted to get it over with.

Looking into the face of the young knight brought a smile to her lips and she forgot all about what lay ahead. Looking into those eyes she saw only the moment and wanted to, oh no, she couldn't even think of it. For some reason the Gods had not granted her a life such as that.

"Ready to go my lady. We'll arrive by evening," said Damon.

"Yes, I am ready," said Amanda.

She wanted to say more but had not the right or the courage. Damon rode ahead, Amanda watching him leave.

"Be careful Mandy. Your looks reveal your thoughts," said Clorisa.

"I know. I will see only the duke once I arrive at the keep. Some people do touch our hearts quickly and he is one," said Amanda.

"Well, I've been taken in by his charm as well," said Clorisa.

"Maybe a double wedding then," said Amanda.

"No, he's too young for me. I'm almost old enough to be his mother."

"Hey, you look ten years younger than you are and he is about twenty-five, so you are even."

"My duty's to you not him."

There it was again Clorisa's talk of duty and no concern about herself. Amanda would have a long talk to her about that when they were settled at the castle. Clorisa had to have a life of her own and Amanda would not take no for and answer. Clorisa's child bearing days would soon run out.

The morning sun disappeared at midday giving way to and iron sky and the roll of thunder in the distant hills. Amanda hoped it was not an omen of things to come but feared it was.

CHAPTER VI

Amanda strained her eyes and in the distance caught the first glimpse of Kara Keep. The two mountains looked as though they were separated by a valley but a stone ridge ran between them. At the top of the stone ridge stood a castle, dark grey towers stretching high. The stone ridge had faces of sheer cliffs; the only way to the top was along a rock path ascending abruptly to the front gate. The steep path was narrow and wound its way to the top with sharp twists in two places. It would be difficult to get siege weapons past those two points.

Sights of the castle made Amanda want to turn and run. It looked so threatening and evil; no love could exist in a place such as this. But that was the intent in its design, to make people want to run rather than attack. The likable knight lived here so there were bound to be others like him, hopefully the duke.

They soon entered the village at the base of the ridge, early evening and no one walked the streets. She didn't expect people to cheer at her arrival but surely someone would be out and about. Curtains moved in windows as eyes peered through the slits, doors came slightly ajar as she rode by. They were watching. What did they have to fear?

"Damon. I had better call you Sir Roth from now on. I

would like to stop and freshen up somewhere before I meet the duke. I do not want him to see me like this," said Amanda.

"Certainly, but may I caution against taking overly long as the ride up the path to the castle is perilous in the dark," said Damon.

They stopped at an inn where she and Clorisa washed then her maid brushed the tangles from her hair. Clothing was touched up as best they could, both having spent the last four days in the same dress. A knock on the door from Damon told them it was time to move on. It would have to do; she would meet her husband to be and he would understand.

Amanda stared in awe at the castle as they rode up the narrow stone path, sheer drops on either side. Sapphire her mare and Clorisa's horse were nervous as they ascended the grade.

"They're a little skittish the first time but they'll soon get used to it," said Damon.

"Is there a path like this on the other side of the ridge," asked Amanda.

"Its double yes," said Damon.

"So the only way in and out of the valley is through the castle," said Amanda.

"Yes that's the idea."

"Are there wells within the castle walls?" asked Amanda.

"Yes, an underground spring not too far down that runs between the two mountains. A clever question my lady but remember I caution you against being that clever inside," said Damon.

"I know I will take care. I will be clever only around you my friend," said Amanda.

Amanda looked for windows in the castle and found none,

only arrow slits not wide enough for a child to climb through. This was definitely a frontier fortress that was built for war and defence with no other purpose in mind. No cosmetics of any kind adorned its surface; only one flag flapped in the gentle wind. It hung on the highest tower with the Huxley crest displayed on it.

One of the two huge gates at the entrance groaned and creaked open before them. Guards stood on either side as Amanda followed Sir Roth into the cobblestone courtyard. Amanda scanned her surroundings and was soon filled with gloom. The place seemed dark and dreary, the guards and soldiers looked like the walking dead. It appeared as though some demon had drained the life out of the entire courtyard. The grey stone had somehow turned black as though cursed. It was evening and maybe all would look brighter by the light of day but tonight Amanda doubted that the sun ever shone in this dismal place. It needed colour and life.

They dismounted before the highest tower and walked toward the front door. Sir Roth hammered at it with the clapper and an elderly gentleman opened it before him.

The old man looked at Clorisa and said, "You must be Lady Daggot, come in please."

"No I'm the maid and this is Lady Daggot."

"Oh, I'm sorry."

"That is all right, many make that mistake," said Amanda cursing her plain look.

"Don't worry we'll fix you up so that you'll shine as soon as we get settled," said Clorisa.

"Where is Duke Huxley? I need to see him for a moment," said Sir Roth.

"He's out hunting. I don't know when he'll be back. Left two days ago," said the servant.

"Who's in charge?"

"Well, he said you are Sir Roth."

"The duke does that, just gets up and leaves. He probably forgot I wasn't even here," said Sir Roth quietly to Amanda.

"Can we go to our rooms?" asked Clorisa.

"Yes, Agnes will take you."

An aged woman took Amanda to a large bedroom containing two beds, dressers, and all the comforts she was used to. Clorisa would stay in the room with her as had always been the case. They shared a room as they shared their lives and work; not because they had to as many rooms lay empty at both castles but because it was convenient. They never fought and that always amazed Amanda as family members especially sisters fought and Clorisa was like a sister. She fought with her father often and Andrew her brother twice as much but never with Clorisa. How could that be?

"Agnes, is there anywhere we can buy new clothing? We had to leave ours behind half way here when we lost our escort," said Amanda.

"Not today. There is a woman in the village that can make whatever you want. For now I'll take you to a room where spare clothes have accumulated for the last few years. They're not new but I'm sure you'll find something," said Agnes.

They followed Agnes two floors up to a room full of closets and attacked the dresses and gowns that were there. Amanda tossed dresses this way and that trying to find just the right thing to wear for her husband to be. She had hoped he would be waiting especially when their arrival had been delayed. And why hadn't he sent out patrols to search for them? Sir

Roth came merely by chance; it was as though all of a sudden the duke no longer cared. Why the haste to bring her here, it didn't make sense.

"What do you think of this one Clorisa?"

"Too light. You look best in a mid shade."

"All right. This one then."

"That's for an old woman not a bride to be."

Finally she found something acceptable and Clorisa agreed. Shoes were found and so was a clean cloak. After a bath she would be ready.

They descended the stairs and Agnes appeared showing them to the dinner table. Sir Roth sat in the duke's chair as he was in charge until his return. Amanda was the guest of honour and would sit at his right. The meal consisted of pork, vegetables, and bread with ale served as the only beverage. No wine or mead was available.

Amanda chewed hard on the gummy pork but was unable to break it down to a point where she could swallow it. She looked across the table to Clorisa who had the same problem. Both gracefully spit the pork into a napkin and dug into the vegetables as they were famished. They must have been prepared yesterday as they were cold and soggy. The bread was hard with crusts of near iron. Amanda was not going to be the lady of the castle and have meals such as this served to the knights and officers. Something was going to change at the keep. She looked at her maid who simply nodded knowing what Amanda was thinking.

They went to their chamber and retired for the night, Amanda asleep as soon as her head hit the pillow. Morning came too soon as Clorisa shook her out of bed. They descended for the morning meal not surprised to find burned porridge waiting. She was not yet Lady of the castle so would have to hold her tongue. She looked at Sir Roth who only smiled.

"I hope you've found all to your liking," said Sir Roth.

"Not really, the food is inedible," Amanda whispered.

"It's always been that way. I usually eat at the village inn," said Sir Roth.

"When I am Lady of the keep all that will change, I can assure you of that," Amanda whispered.

"I don't think it ill will on their part. It's only a lack of knowledge," said Sir Roth.

"Is there a wine cellar here?" asked Amanda.

"Yes but Dione has the only key and she's with the duke."

"Who's Dione?"

"The duke's um, um, mistress, I guess is the only way to state it."

Amanda swallowed hard and rose quickly unable to hide her pain. Tears flowed and her pace quickened as she rushed to the courtyard.

CHAPTER VII

Originally Amanda thought that the duke's haste in demanding the dispatching of his new wife to be was due to the man's loneliness in a northern land. Little by little her original thoughts were being discarded and all was definitely not what she had thought it would be. What was she here for? He wasn't waiting for her, had a woman of his choosing. The only thing left was the dowry, her lands and rental payments from them. If he was free to choose a mistress then maybe she could have an affair with another. Well things didn't work that way. She would be drowned as an unfaithful wife or whatever they do to unfaithful women around here. Her future was in her hands though. She just had to work out the details.

The duke was on his way to the keep so the messenger said. He would be home before dark tonight and all scurried to prepare for his return. Amanda saw the dead come to life in preparation for their master's return. It was fear they laboured under, not love or respect for their lord. Amanda saw that he had some kind of hold over them but believed it was the whip and not words of love they answered to. She was also under his mysterious spell hardly able to control her anxiety at their first meeting. She and Clorisa had done their best with dress and attire, her hair was perfect and her maid had sharpened every detail of her being to utter perfection. If she did not please him or win his favour this day then she never would.

Amanda stood at a narrow arrow slit window in her chamber and looked out to the courtyard below. The sun had sunk below the walls of the keep and light was growing dim. The main gate groaned and creaked open as a dozen riders rode into castle yard. They converged on the duke's palace and entered the door below. She heard the sound of clanging iron and yelling from the entrance hall. Amanda sat on the bed waiting to be invited by the duke to attend him in the great hall.

Amanda sat and waited wringing her hands in apprehension. She pulled threads from her dress and straightened it many times. Clorisa sat at her side stroking her arm gently. Amanda could wait no longer so rose and decided she would seek his audience. She descended to the hall where a dozen men sat drinking ale and telling tales of the hunt. As she entered all were silent, eyes upon her waiting for her to speak. Their look was grim and judgemental; it looked as though each and everyone was planning her demise.

Amanda glanced at the man at the head of the table, a tall man with broad shoulders, dark hair, and beard. His eyes were bright and alive his look appraising. Beside him, in one of his big arms he held a blonde woman, her breasts almost spilling out of her dress, a smirk on her face.

"My name is Amanda Daggot; I believe you have sent for me my lord."

"Yes please be seated here."

A soldier at his left rose from a chair a she sat beside the duke. He still held the blonde in his right arm no change in his look or manner. The evening went on and all acted as though she wasn't there. No one glanced her way or paid any attention to her whatsoever. Amanda felt the discomfort of a mortal among Gods so rose from her chair to exit the hall.

The duke finally spoke of her when she started to rise.

"My wife to be and I will now retire," said Huxley.

Amanda stared into his eyes and said, "I think it a little early as it is not yet our wedding night."

It was the wrong thing to say she could see it in his eyes, they turned dark, the darkest eyes she had ever seen. He could kill with a look such as that, she knew it.

"Get the priest, now," yelled Huxley.

Two of his men rushed away as though their lives lay in the balance. They returned in no time with a priest held between them.

"Marry us now and be quick about it," said Huxley.

Amanda glanced his way seeing his face flushed red and white knuckles on his fisted hands. She meekly sat, quiet as a mouse.

The priest tied her right hand to his left with a cloth of red and said a few words in a language she did not understand. Then in answer to a threatening glance from Huxley, he pronounced them man and wife. All Amanda could think of at that moment was that her wish had come true and it was all over with quickly. No white dress. No flowers. No carriage. There was nothing but a few words from a priest and by the look of him, a drunken priest at that.

Huxley grabbed her hand, dragged her across the floor and up the stairs. Her shins scraped along the stone steps as she failed to keep up. Amanda heard his men laughing in the background and knew she was the evening's entertainment.

He flung open the door to his chamber and tossed her onto the bed.

"Take off your clothes."

Amanda undressed and was down to her shift when she stalled and looked toward him silently begging him to be gentle. He tore her undergarments from her body then stood back looking at her as though she was a prize cow.

"A little skinny and small in places but you'll father my child, so lay back and we'll get on with it."

She lay on the bed as he loomed over her sending surges of fear throughout. Huxley lay over her with a death stare in his eyes. Before the duke did anything else, before he did what she thought the man was going to do. He hit her, fist closed, in the side of her head three or four times. She was almost unconscious but heard him say, "Don't ever say no to me ever again."

Amanda felt him raping her but only in a semi conscious state; then he was gone.

Not long after he came back to his room, the blonde Dione at his side.

"Get the bitch back to her room," said Huxley.

Dione and a servant pulled Amanda to her room where Clorisa waited.

"Oh child, I'm so sorry, I'll kill him I swear," cried Clorisa.

"No, you must not do that," she heard herself say.

Her maid had killed Cabot with not so much as a second thought. She would without doubt kill Huxley as well. Then the king would have both their heads.

She was only partially conscious fighting for comprehension trying to analyze what had taken place. After what he'd done she was amazingly calm. She searched for emotions, not that they were hard to find, only which one to feel first. Tears ran down her cheeks as she searched for ways to blame herself yet found none. She looked for ways to blame him; he was what he was, that's all.

In some strange way it all made sense to her; a conquering soldier taking the spoils of war. Consciousness returned to quickly for her as more emotions assaulted her. There was self pity; but she refused to feel that. Then rage showed its ugly face but rage against a man twice as strong as her was futile at best. Then disappointment struck home. There was no fighting that. She slid from the bed landing on her knees, her forehead touching the floor as uncontrollable tears burst forth. She'd sunk as low as she could and wanted to crawl lower still. She felt Clorisa's touch and heard her friend sob as well.

Amanda's long awaited wedding night was over and had been worse than she could ever have imagined. She drank herb tea that Clorisa brought up from the kitchen as her maid held water soaked cloths to her face. The duke was a fighter, a warrior, and those kinds of men didn't live long; she would just have to wait and outlast him somehow.

One thing for sure she could never mother a child of his. With an heir that would link him to her family and lands she would be dead a week after the baby was born. After bearing his child he could kill her with little suspicion falling on him. It was well known that small boned women did not fare well in the north. They were especially susceptible to certain illness such as pneumonia. After the child was spanked on the bottom and uttered its first cry he could smother her with a pillow and walk away from her lifeless body a rich man. Clorisa knew the ways of herbs and would help her make sure no child of his would grow in her womb.

"You'll have to spend your life with that man," cried Clorisa.

"Yes or until one of us dies."

CHAPTER VIII

Amanda looked into the mirror with one eye as her left was swollen shut. The left side of her face was swollen and her lips cracked. In the chamber pot, she saw her urine was red with blood. Her body was bruised especially around her breasts. She didn't know what he had done to her after the beating but maybe that was a blessing.

Amanda would make no attempt to soften his heart as he lacked one. The knights had warned her of that but she did not know of what they spoke; she did now. They suggested she watch and say nothing but with that one little slip, only words of hesitation, she brought this upon herself. Perhaps the outcome would have been the same had she said nothing. Maybe he wanted to burn into her mind from the start that he was lord and master.

Amanda would stay in her room today and let Clorisa tend to her. Feeling shame and looking beaten she needed time to think. She was not woman enough to avert his actions; not woman enough to change his disdain to acceptance.

Amanda felt guilty and for what? What did she do? No, she was not one of his stupid wenches; she was guilty of nothing. There was no one to turn to however even though she was in the right. The priest would tell her that her lord and master had the right to use her the way he saw fit. She was to submit, honour, and obey.

The duke didn't come to her that night, not out of shame or regret. She would bet her inheritance on that. He probably wanted to spend the night with his blonde wench. Clorisa made an herb tea for her that would help her sleep and kill the pain. She would also give her an herb drink after supper that would render his seed useless in her womb when he preformed his cruel version of love making. Amanda would have to take it daily and never forget; her life was at stake.

The next morning she surveyed the damages; her face was still swollen, lips still split, and her urine was still red. What if her lord and master did this every time he came to her? She would have to hide in this room and forsake the outside world. By now everyone knew what had happened. They would wonder what kind of woman she was, a timid flower or a fighter.

"Come Clorisa we have a castle to manage. Let us start by teaching the cooks how to prepare a proper meal."

"Yes my lady."

"No, never that, it's Amanda."

"Yes, Amanda."

As soon as Amanda descended the stairway Agnes appeared as though in waiting. The look on her face when she saw the swelling and half shut eye revealed her true feelings. She felt Agnes's hand on her arm; Agnes was on her side. They went to the kitchen and Amanda was not surprised to see the place a mess; grease and remnants of long ago meals lay everywhere. It was a miracle the place had not yet been devoured by flames. There were pot hooks on the walls but not one pot hung there.

They were all stacked on counters and even set in corners on the floor, no one cared.

Amanda and Clorisa as though of one mind rolled up their sleeves and started to work. First they scooped the remnants of food and grease into buckets and carried them to the compost outside. The kitchen staff of four as though out of shame, one by one started to help. Water was boiled pots were cleaned the hearth where the cooking was done, scrubbed. Agnes had disappeared but returned with the chimney sweep that would scrape the grease from deep inside the hearth.

That evening Clorisa instructed the staff how to prepare the evening meal. Amanda was already looking about the rest of the castle and found her way to the courtyard in early evening. It looked the way she saw it that first night, dismal and gloomy, even the men walking the ramparts looked lifeless. One man almost stumbled and she knew then that he was drunk. She watched as Sir Roth walked her way. Amanda wanted to but was unable to run. She would have to face him sooner or later. For some reason this man mattered to her, meant more to her than he should. Her husband was like the captain of her escort, a bully and a thug. Huxley belonged here in this place but what was this kind knight doing here?

"Good day my lady."

Amanda turned her swollen face trying to hide the damage, "Good day kind sir. Is it folly on my part or are those men on the ramparts drunk?"

"They're drunk I'm afraid."

"How? Where are they getting it?"

"The wine cellar where all drink is stored is never locked."

"Who would I see about having it locked?"

"I'll tend to it."

"I need it opened for the evening meal. The soldiers can have their rations at that time also. Two cups per man."

"Consider it done. Anything else?"

"No that is all thank you."

"Oh my lady, there are a lot of good men here. Don't judge all by the actions of a few."

"I will always take your advice good friend although it may look to you that I did not."

Sir Roth smiled as though to be polite and walked away. She watched him out of the corner of her eye until he disappeared then dropped her head and wept into her hands.

Amanda dressed for dinner and entered the great hall. Her seat at the duke's right side was occupied by the blonde, Dione. The woman could have him. Amanda was not here to dine but to make sure dinner went as she had intended. Clorisa was in the kitchen overseeing the kitchen staff. They had co-ordinated their efforts in this way at both of her father's castles. Three of the kitchen staff brought baskets of meat and bread; a pot of soup was also set upon a stand and bowls were filled starting with the duke. She would assist and ask all if there were any special requests that could be tended to. During and after the meal nothing but compliments flowed from the guests. They were the high ranking soldiers and their wives who attended dinner here every night.

Amanda dared not look directly at her husband but the first sign of her brought a scowl to his face. Her mere presence seemed to torment him and she knew another beating was on the way before the last had even healed. Well so be it, she would not cower in some corner. Huxley would not kill her anyway, not before she gave him an heir. He had to have a link to the vast holdings she had inherited. Her death before such an heir was born would nullify her father's contract and no more money would flow his way. Amanda could not fight him and win so would outthink him. He picked the wrong opponent for a battle of wits.

Dinner was finished and went well, all the officer's wives rose one by one to thank her for such a fine feast. Compliments of Clorisa's fine cakes were also included. She would win over the wives and probably some of the officers at the supper table. Amanda went to the kitchen where Clorisa and she had their meal along with the kitchen staff. This is the way they won the loyalty and respect of the staff at the other castles, by being one of them and taking their meals with the staff whenever possible.

That night a knock sounded on her bedroom door and when Amanda opened it was not surprised to see Dione standing before her. The duke wanted her in his bed chamber. She followed and entered her husband already undressed. The door shut behind her and she wondered if Dione's ear would be upon it so opened it and sure enough the blonde stood there, a dumb look on her face. Amanda couldn't blame her; she had a good thing here until he tired of her at least.

"Take off your clothes," said Huxley.

"Yes dear husband but please listen to this before you act. If you ever desire to beat me again then take your dagger and plunge it through my heart because if you do not, I will. I will take my own life rather than let a thug like you beat me the rest of my days."

Amanda watched him stiffen in a rage; his neck muscles tightened and looked like ropes running down to his shoulder. He was clearly unable to speak. He looked like he wanted to kill. She said no more and did not look into his eyes. Amanda wasn't stupid enough to push her luck. This was as far as she could go without losing her life.

She stared into the fire burning in his hearth and waited for a response.

"You're still my wife and will fulfill your obligations to me and provide me with sons."

"If that is your wish then so is it."

Amanda undressed and lay in his bed legs spread limp as she could be. Clorisa's herbs would kill the pain and his seed. She could handle him sexually every night if need be; her body would toughen in the right places. When he was through she dressed and opened the door, Dione was waiting not far down the hall.

Amanda slept well that night. Everyone knew where they stood.

CHAPTER IX

Winter's coming was delayed by an abnormal heat wave that left everyone panting. In the heat of the summer the soldier's wives would load the children in the back of a supply wagon and a picnic would be had at a small lake half a day away from the keep. They could cool off in the icy water and then eat in the shade of surrounding trees.

Plans had been made to do that with Amanda and Clorisa supplying the food. They would both ride along and enjoy the day in the company of the women. There was an escort of ten men to protect them should they run into stray bandits which rarely happened south of the ridge.

It was the first time since Amanda arrived over a week ago that she was able to ride Sapphire. The little mare as well as Clorisa's mount were ready to fly as they both struggled to keep the horses at a walk down the sloping path. Once down and past the village they let their horses run off a weeks worth of oats. Well down the road toward the lake they sat in the shade and waited for the wagon to catch up.

"Do you think the duke will let things be the way they are?" asked Clorisa.

"I think for now yes as he awaits signs of a child. When he does not see those signs, well I do not know. He is a man of passion and violence which is a deadly mixture. He is also a man with no morals so need not justify anything to him or others. He needs the income from my lands. That however is the reason I still live."

"It's impossible to think like him isn't it? So it's hard to plan in advance as you can't possibly know what he will do," said Clorisa.

"We are unlike him burdened with morals and I use the word burdened only because it is such when dealing with a man like him. We are restricted to doing what we can live with giving him the advantage."

"We'll have to stay alert. We may have help though if we need it. I think there are a few standing on your side, like the knight," said Clorisa.

"In the end the duke is the absolute law here; the knight is honour bound to serve him."

"We've lost one advantage though," said Clorisa.

"What is that?"

"He knows you're clever."

"Let us forget about our troubles and enjoy the day."

The wagon caught up and they proceeded to the lake, horses rustling through the leaves. At the lake children screamed and the women laid down blankets setting baskets of food on them waiting for the children to finish their swim.

An arrow whistled through the air and a soldier fell to the ground. Clorisa was the first to notice and alerted the others. The women raced to fetch the children from the water as the men set up a line of defence using trees and the wagon. There were roughly thirty men of the northern tribes. Arrows sunk into trees but still only one dead so far.

The soldiers strung their own bows and fired arrows at the assaulting tribesmen, Gales as they were called. Two of the

Gales were killed before they called off the attack and gathered as though deciding what to do next. In the camp the women had all the children dressed and kneeling behind the wagon and trees. They were outnumbered three to one and no patrols were due until the next day which would be too late.

Amanda looked at the captain of the guard, "Someone has to go out there and get help. I have the fastest horse it will be me that will go."

"No, you're the lady of the castle," said the captain of the guard.

"I will not be for long if we do not get help. I am going and that is all there is to it," said Amanda.

"I won't allow it. One of the men will go."

"On Sapphire I am the fastest rider here. Look at the plough horses you ride," said Amanda. It only made sense.

"An arrow will stop you no matter how fast your mount."

"Well I will just have to stay low and out of range then."

"Oh be careful girl. But I know you're right," said Clorisa.

"I'll try to draw some of them away from you as I go," said Amanda.

Amanda started to mount Sapphire but knew she would be restricted in her thick wool dress so removed it and stood before them only wearing her shift. She mounted and pushed Sapphire into a gallop head low hoping no arrow would find her. The soldiers would be shooting at the Gales to keep their heads down until she cleared.

The Gales pursued. Out of arrow range Amanda slowed slightly to make them think they could catch her. She was trying to draw as many as she could from the women and children at the lake. There were six or so, some crossing the meadows trying to cut her off. Amanda had to get to the keep before the soldiers at the lake ran out of arrows. When they did they would surely be overrun.

The Gales were starting to close on her so she pushed Sapphire into a dead run. Only two were near and one in particular knew how to ride. Amanda glanced at him as he drew his sword. She ducked and turned Sapphire left to avoid his blade as he swung. Through the forest she rode with the man in chase, ducking branches and jumping logs.

Amanda was pinned between a row of pine and the Gale as he burst forward and swung his giant broadsword. She pulled Sapphire to an abrupt stop, the rider shooting by. She turned right toward the road and started toward the keep but he was already ahead of her, waiting. He'd put away his sword and had his bow in hand, an arrow nocked, aiming her way. She caught a glimpse of it before it stung in her left shoulder above her heart. The pain almost drove her from the saddle when she broke off the shaft. He was nocking another arrow so she pushed Sapphire into a dead run. She bent low as she flashed by him. She felt no pain so knew that this arrow missed. Amanda raced toward the keep; he would not catch her now.

The village soon came into view and Amanda turned to check behind, no one was there. She rode through the village and up the path to the keep, the huge gate opening before her. Sir Roth was in sight so she yelled at him.

"The soldiers with women and children are under attack at the lake. Follow me, hurry please, they can't hold out much longer."

She saw soldiers racing toward the stables so would ride back to the lake, they could follow. Her shoulder felt cold but did not ache, only a numbness spreading throughout her entire left side. Amanda felt light headed but had to get back to the others.

Amanda felt more than light headed and gripped tight to the saddle not trusting her feet in the stirrups alone. The road ahead looked blurry yet she felt no pain, only a chill throughout. The lake was almost in sight so she stopped Sapphire to look around. In the distance Amanda saw blurry figures still outside the parameter the soldiers were guarding. She looked over her shoulder and saw her brave knight coming, soldiers close behind.

Amanda fell out of the saddle and looked toward the sky, growing dimmer by the second.

It was a strange world Amanda was in, not of the living, yet not of the dead. It was a half world somewhere in between. She heard voices, Clorisa's above all. She was chanting; she'd heard it before. Amanda saw light and tried to speak but her throat felt dry and cracked. She looked into Clorisa's eyes and started to weep.

"It's all right, you're safe now. Here try to drink a little water."

Clorisa put a cup to her lips and she drank but almost choked. After five or six attempts water finally went down. Amanda could feel it flow right to her stomach as though she hadn't drunk in days.

"How long have I been laying here?" she rasped.

"Four days."

"What? Why?"

"The Gale's rusty arrowhead poisoned your blood. I know of an herb that fights the infection and usually wins."

"Where did you learn all these things?"

"My mother was a healer."

Clorisa went to the kitchen and returned with soup and a certain knight that had been waiting in the front hall for four days for a certain young lady to wake.

"Good day my lady, I'm glad to see you're better. The women and children are all safe thanks to you and only two more soldiers died when driving off the Gales. They thank you all and so do I," stuttered Sir Roth.

Amanda smiled as she had never seen him make even the slightest error in grammar.

"It was for my own life as well. I did not want to die there either."

"Yes and that's why you rode back to them wounded. No that was the bravest thing I have ever seen anyone do and I am a man of war. I bow to you. I pledge my life to you and my king."

Amanda forced back tears and said, "I think you overestimate me but thank you for your praise. Please visit more often. Now tell me what you know of these Gales, there has to be a way to stop the bloodshed."

"I am at your disposal in this matter and whatever else you need."

They talked for a time then Agnes and the staff dropped by one by one to wish her well. Clorisa brought another bowl of soup to replace the one that cooled while visitors attended her. She fell asleep soon after and awoke early next morning. Clorisa dressed her and she walked a few steps around the room then sat upon the bed. The duke never dropped by although she could hear his voice in the hall. He had been out hunting when the attack took place. He would view her ride as a risky venture that could have cost him dearly if she'd died.

Amanda ate the morning and noon meals in her room but decided to attend the great hall for dinner. If not to eat at least to chat with the women she had been with the day of the picnic almost a week ago. It would be old news by now and everyone would be talked out so she would not have to face an embarrassing barrage of sentiment.

Clorisa helped her down the stairs and held her arm as she entered the hall. All seats were taken save one at the other end of the table opposite the duke. She learned later that this was to be her chair. Every officer and knight had agreed it would be so. She stopped and smiled then everyone accept the duke and his wench rose to their feet and clapped, all uttering various words of praise. The duke and Dione left the hall and went who knew where. And who cared.

The dinner went quite well without the unruly duke and his wench. Amanda was relieved when the subject of conversation changed from her efforts at the lake to the children. The women talked of the effect that day had on their loved ones. They talked of the lack of a priest to console and guide the youngsters. The cleric that had married Amanda and the duke went south at the start of the heat wave on Huxley's orders. He had sent the priest on far away missions before.

Amanda looked toward Sir Roth as often as she could without raising suspicion. He in turn would meet her eyes and in those brief seconds she had felt closer to him than any other man before. Amanda wanted that man at the end of the night like nothing she had ever desired. All too soon they were on their own everyone having retired for the night. Reluctantly she departed, filled with both love and disappointment not knowing which was greater. She retired for the night, Clorisa already asleep.

One thing worried Amanda and that was the duke's pride. She was becoming as popular as him and that would not sit well with a man like that. The world revolved around him and if it did not do so he would force it to. Huxley left the dinner table in a childish fit of jealousy because he'd had to share attention with his wife. There would be a point where his pride would override the money factor and he would kill her. That would become harder as time went by if she gathered more allies than he did. Today at least he needed her more than she needed him. Amanda could run the castle without him; hopefully he'd not figured that out yet.

Next morning the sound of horses clattering across the stones of the castle yard brought Amanda to the arrow slot window in her room. The duke was taking his knights and horse mounted troops through the north gate. The south gate was also open as knights ascended the path and rode through the castle from the stables below. Over a hundred men passed to the northlands.

Amanda looked for Sir Roth but unable to find him raced to the stable and found his horse gone, he was with them. She ran to the castle and upstairs to her husband's bed chamber. Dione was still in bed but not asleep.

"Where are they going?" asked Amanda.

"They're going to raid the camps of the Gales in return for their attack on us."

"How did the Gales get to the lake in the first place?"

"Another pass half a day south. It's rough but you can walk a horse through. They look for hostages that they can sell back to us."

"How long will they be gone?"

"As long as it takes, I guess."

Amanda would wait but not for the duke. If he was lost in battle she would be free of him and was now almost ashamed of those thoughts; almost until she remembered the beating. Amanda worried about Sir Roth and did not think she could go on without him. Where did that thought come from? Had she fallen in love with the knight?

Amanda pondered those thoughts and yearned to see his face and gaze into his eyes, wanted to hold him and never let go. All of those dreams that she had before pushed out of her mind descended upon her now as his life lay in peril. Time ground to a halt, her mind empty; even Clorisa said little as though knowing of her sad predicament.

Two days later the alarm bells rang bringing Amanda to the courtyard. The gates groaned and squeaked while opening wide. The duke rode through them, his troops close behind. He dismounted and walked past her not saying a word, only contempt in his eyes. His soldiers rode through the courtyard and out the south gate to the valley below.

The wounded came last, her Knight Sir Roth being among them. The knight's head hung low, his right arm limp at his side. Amanda ran to him trying to help him from his horse. Wearing his armour and weapons his weight brought her to her knees. Clorisa was soon at her side helping to carry him through the castle doors. Once inside Agnes told them there were no rooms to spare as the wounded occupied all.

"We will take him to my bed chamber," said Amanda.

"What will the duke say? Take care, don't push him too far." said Clorisa.

"Clorisa, I need you to care for him as you would me and let me worry about the duke."

"All right, come on Agnes and help us get him upstairs," said Clorisa.

They stripped him of armour and clothes then Clorisa washed his wounds and stitched the deepest cuts. The flesh in his right arm was laid bare to the bone as was his right leg.

"Listen to me child, I know how much you care for him but I will tell you no lies. His wounds are severe and infection has taken hold. If he lives through this night it will be by the grace of the Gods and not for what I have done. I will do what I can but have not the magic to save his life so pray as nothing else can save him now," said Clorisa.

"Leave the door open and we will both tend to him through the night. A man almost dead and you here as well there is nothing the duke can say," said Amanda.

Amanda thought only of his first name Damon as she stroked his brow with cold towels. There was nothing to do but pray and keep his body cool while the fever burned within. Clorisa mixed one herb with the next, measuring and concentrating as she had never seen her do before.

Clorisa said words in a language foreign to Amanda as the mixtures foamed and boiled within the cup. She poured the smoking liquid into his mouth little by little as it slowly ran down his throat. Clorisa chanted and raved as Amanda slammed the door shut.

Amanda had seen women burned at the stake for less.

The night dragged on as Clorisa soaked in sweat said the same incoherent words over and over again. After an eternity of sweat and worry the morning sun lit the room and Sir Roth was still alive; just barely yet he lived. Clorisa lay as though lifeless on the floor, Amanda refused to stop praying and stroking his brow.

At midday Clorisa came to and examined the knight. She smiled and looked content.

"He's through the worst of it and sleeps sound. The herbs did their work. The knight is strong as well. Get some sleep I'll tend to him," said Clorisa.

After his near death Amanda knew for certain she loved Damon Roth. She had not known him for long yet felt more certain of him than any other man she had ever met not counting Gibbin. Damon was like an island in a raging sea. It wasn't only that she wanted him, he was a desirable man. She needed him, needed his approval, his company, and most of all his love. She had always considered herself strong and could cope with whatever came her way. He fulfilled her heart and soul in ways she never knew existed.

Amanda smiled thinking of her first puppy. Life was grand before Candy, that little ball of fur, came along but twice as grand when she opened her heart to that little dog. Damon was a hundred times grander than that.

There was a knock on the door and Clorisa answered. It was a fellow knight, Sir Benton, best friend to Sir Roth or so he said. She had to watch herself, never knew who the duke's spies were.

"How is he doing?"

"His health is still in peril, but he has a chance now," said Clorisa.

"It was all so unnecessary if the duke had let the archers do their work. The duke rushed in before a single arrow had left a bow. He attacked as a madman and forced the knights to enter the battle in his defence while the enemy numbers were great. Three knights died and two were wounded for his folly," said Sir Benton.

Amanda had none but disdain for her husband after hearing another's account. She wanted to kill him and get this fool out of her life and everyone else's. She went to the great hall where he sat surrounded by his captains. They all cheered his bravery and cunning in the demise of the tribesmen they encountered. The attention given her after what she had done at the lake now reverted back to him. Huxley was a true warrior after all and knew what was required to get the attention of men, so did that at the cost of others.

Sir Benton told her of things they had done to the enemy no pride in his voice only disdain. They had burned the enemy's winter food supply and huts. Most would not see the spring and would perish; women and children would die first. That would stoke the fires of hate making the Gales seek revenge the following year and so the cycle would continue.

Amanda knew that peace had to prevail; the slaughter would have to end. She had only one chance and that was through the leader of the northern tribes. If he was like her husband then they would be doomed to a life of eternal war. She needed to know more about the lands and people in order to reverse the current tide.

CHAPTER X

Winter returned with savage fury as the first snow put an end to the heat wave. The world was white as Amanda and Clorisa descended to the village below. Amanda had learned that only one hundred soldiers lived within the keep. Three hundred more lived in the village and farms around the base of the castle as far as one day south. Only sixty horses were kept in the stable on the grounds of the keep. These could be used by the knights and mounted troops in an emergency as they had at the lake.

Hay was hoisted daily by a huge winch from the floor of the cliff that the castle sat upon. Manure was disposed of over the edge at a point farther along the castle wall. Oats and grain were also lifted as were supplies needed for human consumption. Cattle were butchered below and the meat lifted to the keep above. In this way the castle was supplied with food and the waste removed.

Under a siege the rules changed; the horses were let go and the castle stores of salted meat and grain rationed. Soldiers would flee the village and farms and seek sanctuary within the safety of those grey walls. Water would not be a problem as wells within were spring fed. The hundred men within could hold off an invasion force of a thousand.

Sir Roth was on his way to recovery as he worked with

the arms master daily. His right arm was almost of no use and his right leg was only half as strong as his left. He wielded his sword in his left hand but was clumsy to say the least. His determination quelled all fears in Amanda's mind as he worked to overcome his weakness.

Today however she did not seek an answer to her fears or losses, she sought the house of the horse master Ely. He was in charge of the four hundred horses that were housed in pastures around the village. He had a daughter, Ellen known by the villagers as the Princess of horses, a rider equalled by none. Amanda was the winner of every race at every fair held in her land on Sapphire and had to meet her equal here in the north.

With the help of directions by Agnes she arrived at the farm, Clorisa at her side as usual. The idea of going anywhere without her maid never entered her mind. Both dismounted and knocked upon the door of the horse master. His wife answered and they were directed to the paddocks and buildings.

The man stood out like a knight among pages, giving orders that made young men scramble left and right.

"Hello, I'm the duchess, Amanda. Could I look around? I am a lover of horses and heard you were the best trainer we have."

"Certainly my lady. What would you like to see?"

"You have a daughter Ellen. I have heard much about her and would like to meet her if possible."

"Why yes of course, I'll fetch her."

Not much later he returned with a young woman, beautiful in a rough way, her dark hair tied back, a gleam in her brown eyes.

"Yes my lady. How may I serve?"

"May we ride together? I wish to see our farmland."

"Yes, I'll saddle my horse."

She returned not much later with her legendary stallion Shamus at the end of her reins. This was no plough horse and a hand higher than Sapphire, showing a lot more muscle than her mare.

They mounted and rode through the country side, a champion from the south next to a champion from the north. A contest had been declared the minute they met and was waiting to be played out. Each awaited a cue from the other, a word, a phrase, a movement, something that would signal the start of a race.

Amanda put an end to the tension, "I will race you to those trees near the mountain base."

Both were off, their horses responding as if their riders were but a load to test each other with. Both horse competed against each other and ignored the weight upon their backs. They raced through the snow and over the road, across the meadow and toward the trees beyond. Nose to nose they ran neither giving way to the other; girl against boy in the never ending battle within nature. The girl won by a nose but only a nose, it could have gone either way.

"I need you with me Ellen. On my side if you will. Please attend me at court if it be in your heart to do so. The choice is yours. I will not force you. I need your skill as a rider and your knowledge of the people and this land. Please join my side," said Amanda.

"I don't know of what help I can be and I have my work here. I'll speak with father about it though."

It was the land surrounding the castle that Amanda would use to turn Kara Keep from loss to profit. She would bring sheep to this land from her farms in the south. Only a few families would have to be brought here to teach the villagers the making of wool. A trade route would be established and soldiers would maintain peace along the way. All this she would do if her husband didn't kill her first.

Amanda needed Ellen to oversee the sheep farming venture she was setting in motion this spring. Ellen knew animals, people, and most importantly the land. Her father Ely had a full time job as horse master and she could ask no more of him.

Amanda had been only thirteen when her mother taught her the ways of farming, of profit and loss. Her mother saw it as a matter of survival to stay as far ahead of starvation as humanly possible. There were many obligations which had to be met. She was taught to serve those that served her and create a continuing cycle that would benefit all.

Amanda was delighted when Ellen arrived at the castle of her own free will. She would not force her into anything but needed her as no other here would do. Amanda explained what she intended to do and told Ellen of her part.

Ellen was speechless at first then her eyes went wide and said, "I cannot do it. I have no knowledge of such things."

"You will have help. I know it appears a great task but I would not ask if I did not think you capable."

"Who'll look after the sheep out there among the wolves?"

"A shepherd and his dogs. Dogs do most of the work, herding and looking after sheep. It is easy once started. The only hard part is shearing and I will bring people here to teach that art."

"I don't know. I fear I'll let you down."

"Try it please, you will see it as a step by step matter and if you do not want to continue at any time then come and see me; I will have to find another."

"I'll talk to my father and see what he says. He knows more of the world than I and really need his council in this matter."

Amanda let Ellen return to her world hoping she would help. Amanda needed her.

The next day her husband came to her in a rage, "You're not going to turn my knights into shepherds, this is a place for warriors."

"Why do you think the King paired us? You are a warrior and I a woman of business. He cannot sustain you forever. We are going to have to learn to fend for ourselves. Warriors and shepherds will both be welcome here or none at all."

"The King has no choice but to finance this castle as it is all that keeps the Gales from his back door."

"He can easily drop this line of defence back to Barkley Castle. They are self sufficient and have as many soldiers as you."

"I warn you, keep your shepherds out of my way. I'll slay the first one that sets foot in this castle."

Amanda said no more and would let the duke mull over his changing role. It was another reason for him to kill her.

Only a week before he'd called her a barren, cold bitch because she'd had her monthly courses. It infuriated him to a point where she feared for her life. He'd not had her brought to his bed chamber and this was the first meeting since then.

Sir Roth was improving and would meet her in the great hall when both knew the duke and Dione were absent. It was a public spot with Clorisa present where she could not be accused of infidelity. If he could prove disloyalty she would be drowned and he would still have the rights to her land despite the fact that he openly had a mistress. Her children would have to be clean born as the contract stated or declared bastards and left at the hands of her lord and master, the duke.

The next day Ellen returned. At other times when Amanda had seen the young lady she was dressed in riding clothes and smelled of hay and horses. It wasn't as though Amanda minded that as she was often in the same state but today there was a definite change. Ellen's dark hair flowed free and long it was, almost to her lower back. She wore a dress that touched the floor and smelled of lotions and scents. Her manner was stiff and awkward as she appeared uncomfortable and unsure of herself.

"Good day my lady."

"Good day Ellen and call me Amanda."

"I've spoken to my father and he wants me to help you anyway I can. He says trade will be good for our people."

"What do you want to do?"

"I too wish to help you. Anyone who would take upon themselves a great chore as you have will have my blessing and aid."

"The first thing we need is a peace treaty with the Gales. Who would I see about meeting with them?"

"Melanie the village healer was one of them until she came to us years ago. You'll find her in the inn most days."

"We will ride south at the first sign of spring. For now organize some help from the village, they will be paid from this day forward. Twenty men will do for now. You will handle the money. I will pay a silver coin per week. I will give you ten gold coins per week."

"No that's too much, my father doesn't make that."

"But you will and you will feel it is not enough when we start to work in the spring."

"I'll hire the men."

"And start building simple huts in the lands past the lake. There is not much snow around so it should be possible. We will need shelter for shepherds in those hills."

Amanda had not turned all her money over to the duke. He had no idea the vast wealth under her control and she hoped he never would. With all her money he would hire mercenaries and kill as many Gales as he could find, causing more problems in the long run than he could control. The king had left half her assets out of the contract and she suspected the king knew more than he would say. The king had left her enough money to do what she was doing now and wondered if it had been his thought from the start. Her husband was a threat to her plan so she would see Sir Roth and enlist his help. The knight needed new work in any case as the duke had removed him from his post as first knight after his injury. Sir Roth had announced that he would leave in the spring and return to the King's court in the south.

Sir Roth's entrance to the great hall put a smile on Amanda's lips. His injury only fuelled the love she had for him; his limp made him somehow more human.

"Good day first knight."

"Not anymore I'm afraid; it's more like last knight now."

"To me you'll always be the first knight," said Amanda and it's all she would say out loud as the duke's spies might be about.

"Clorisa told me you had something important to speak to me about, please tell."

"To start with I will tell you that I am going to turn Kara Keep from a military castle into a farming endeavour as well. The hilly rocky land will best support sheep and an industry in wool. I need your services in the area of maintaining law not only here but for the trade route south," said Amanda and waited for a reply.

"You are a woman of vision, that is certain. You will have whatever help a crippled knight can give."

Amanda shivered hearing those words of self pity from a man of such strength and character. Had Huxley somehow destroyed his self worth in declaring another first knight? She hesitated not knowing how to proceed as a knight's honour lay at stake.

"I ask this of you not out of pity, I ask it because you are the one I need. If there were another more suited to the task then I would ask him. You are my friend whether you chose to help or decline," whispered Amanda.

She looked at Damon, her first knight and first love as he froze at sound of her words. His eyes and body were unreadable as he stared back at her as though expecting to hear more.

Then with a shake of his head said, "You honour me dear lady and more than that you touch my soul. I will tell you then that I've loved you as a friend since first we met, since first I gazed into your eyes and touched your soul. I pledge my life to you and King in that order," whispered Sir Damon Roth.

Amanda forced back tears and swallowed hard. She wanted to attack him and kiss lips, such were her thoughts. She refrained knowing it would mean death for both.

"Dear Damon we go forth this day as one. No vows can be spoken no priest sanctions our union, only you and

I and of course Clorisa bear witness to our bond," whispered Amanda.

Amanda watched as he chocked back his emotions, "I must be going dear lady as I have work that needs to be done."

Damon left the great hall with a limp yet rising taller with every stride. She watched every step and ached for him to turn back but knew deep within he would not. He would protect her in every way forsaking his own desires that much she knew.

Amanda and Clorisa went to the village in search of Melanie the village healer. Ellen's words were without fault as they found the healer at the inn. If rumour be true then she was a sorceress but Amanda doubted the accuracy of that statement. The priest would have long ago burned her at the stake if he had proof of such claims. Watching her within the bar Amanda concluded that Melanie did possess a gift; she had power over men. All soldiers drunk or sober greeted her trying to gain her favour.

Amanda and Clorisa approached her, "Hello, I am Amanda and this is Clorisa. May we speak?"

"Of course, I'm Melanie and I know you to be the duchess and you Clorisa, the healer."

"I need your help. Ellen told us you may be able to get word to Rogun. I wish to speak to him of a peace treaty. One that would work in his favour. I would like him to at least hear what I have to say."

"Well yes my lady, I'll tell him. Whether he sees you or not is another matter not under my control."

"That is all I ask."

"Do you not think it of great danger meeting with the leader of the heathens?" asked Melanie.

"All life is a risk. I share my bed with one who would slay me after my first born. So it would seem Rogun and I have a common enemy. Let it be known that I serve my King, not my husband."

"And what makes your King different?"

"He seeks peace."

"I will leave tomorrow. It may be a few days before I return."

Clorisa and Melanie swapped herbs formulas the way cooks exchanged recipes. Amanda had taken another step toward her eventual plan. She quivered with excitement and hoped all would go as planned.

CHAPTER XI

A mid winter rain washed away most of the snow. Amanda and Clorisa left the castle that morning following Melanie south to a pass which would take them to the lands of the Gales. Melanie had returned after an eight day absence and told her Rogun would see her. They could not take the north gate from the castle as Huxley would send soldiers to bring them back. They would be gone for a few days but once gone no one would know in which direction to search. Once their business was concluded and if still alive they would make up tales of being lost in the wilderness. Amanda could care less what the duke thought.

They dismounted and walked their horses along the rough trail. A slip here would send them scrambling across rough stones. They mounted on the other side of the pass and rode north to where Rogun awaited.

All searched for dry wood as the last light of day followed the sun under the earth. The fire was started then Clorisa prepared warm drinks then soup for all. The horses were hobbled and grazed quietly not far away.

Clorisa noticed them first as she always did. She had an uncanny sense of her surroundings. When a child Amanda could never surprise her, she always knew when Amanda snuck up behind.

"We're not alone," said Clorisa.

"I feel them to," said Melanie.

"Who or what?" said Amanda.

"You're right woman, you're not alone," spoke a low rough voice out of the dark.

"Rogun, come here. We're only three women. We won't hurt you," said Melanie.

"I know," said the big man coming into view. He wore clothes of cloth not animal skins as Amanda had been told, from his waist hung a broadsword and a dagger. His long hair and shaggy beard hid all save his brow and eyes. He sat on the log next to Melanie then looked into Amanda's eyes.

"You have an offer of peace for me after burning my crops and homes."

"I seek not to debate injustices done in the past as I myself arrived shortly before this winter. I will only speak of what I wish to do, the dreams I have for this land. I cannot undo the past, only hope we can build a better future."

"What do you offer?"

"Two hundred gold coins today as a sign of good faith. You can ride to the coast and purchase grain for the winter. In the spring I will drive a hundred sheep to you. You can butcher them or raise them for wool as we will do."

"Who will control the duke?"

"I will attend the King in the spring and ask him to intervene. It will not be easy kind sir as there will be more trouble to come. I ask you to work with me. Melanie will be our common voice and through her I hope to achieve a lasting peace."

"If I see Huxley gone or under control then we'll have an agreement. He's the only one who stands in the way."

"I know, believe me I know."

Amanda gave Rogun the purse containing two hundred gold coins which he reluctantly accepted.

"I don't accept charity but I will take the coins as they will save the lives of many I love. I'll look upon it as a loan and repay you next summer," said Rogun.

"I think we will have a good relationship Rogun," said Amanda with a smile.

Amanda and Clorisa returned to the castle with tales of being lost. Amanda suspected they all knew it was a lie. Where they had gone would remain a mystery. She knew it would drive Huxley mad.

Amanda talked to Sir Roth often in the great hall planning their ride south in the spring. Her knight would ride with them to a point then head east to the King's palace. He would seek the King's council in regards to the problems of Kara Keep.

Amanda watched Sir Roth practice with the arms master in the main yard. He was finally mastering the sword in his left hand putting the arms master on his toes. His speed and strength increased day by day. She could see why this man was a knight, his heart and prowess with weapons was beyond the norm.

The winter edged forward as most do, a storm followed by a mild spell then another three days of storms. Men and animals sought shelter, the occupants of the keep and village enjoyed the fruits of their labour consuming goods they had spent the summer working to store. There was sufficient grain for the people and enough hay for the horses. Meat was supplemented by the hunting parties from the keep; sometimes plenty and sometimes none. They were far from starvation or lack of ale. The brew masters had been extremely busy this year.

Winter was alive with the visits of others and gatherings of all sorts. The young made love and the elderly sought comfort in the company of one another. The keep survived another season of nature's wrath on beast and mankind.

Amanda had more to endure than the others as the duke blamed the snow and cold of winter on her as though only the sun shone until she arrived. He cursed her monthly courses and called her barren and cold. He would have killed her merely out of boredom if he could, if he could have afforded the loss.

Her meetings with her love Sir Roth were less frequent as the duke and Dione were home more often during this season of storms. Amanda spent most of her time in longing, for his voice, merely to gaze into his eyes. The winter winds could not end swift enough for her as she awaited the warming breath of spring.

CHAPTER XII

The days grew longer and the sun higher in the sky as spring warmed the icy breath of winter. A dozen riders wearing the Daggot crest rode into Kara Keep. Amanda's heart pounded at their arrival knowing the meaning urgent. A Daggot soldier told her that her father passed away two weeks before.

Amanda and Clorisa hugged and cried, both feeling the loss. Amanda had never been close to her father as business matters had dominion over all else. He'd signed the contracts that put her in Huxley's hands. For all his faults, he was still her father and now dead would miss someone she had never known in life. There were no memories of family times, like horseback rides in the country with her mother. Her father was always too busy to attend family events yet seemed to have ample time for his colleagues. Amanda searched for a loving moment shared with her father yet found not a single one. The one feeling he had given her was one of belonging; she was the daughter of the Duke and may the Gods help anyone who forgot that. He did give her that.

Amanda could not help taking her eyes off Clorisa. Her maid servant had been sobbing all day long.

"You are taking father's death more seriously then I am. You had an affair with him did you not?"

Clorisa looked her way, eyes red as though in apology,

"After your mother died we were both distraught needing each other's company. One thing led to another then one night I found myself in his bed."

"My mother just fresh in the grave?"

"It wasn't planned. It just happened but not for long. After I got over the initial loss I felt like I was betraying a dear friend by bedding your father. So it ended as quickly as it began, the affair born of love for your mother, nothing more.

"I was devastated by her death. I didn't think I could go on without her help and guidance. She'd been there for me all those years pulling me out of a back alley, half starved when I was younger than you. She made me what I am today."

"Did father love mother?"

"Oh yes. Men like him don't take easily to people but once they do.. There were good years between them when you were but a child."

"What happened?"

"Time, business, and most of all pressure on your parents from the king. You must always bare in mind that a monarch has the power to hang any man he chooses for treason if his demands are not met. It's not easy as you've found being born of nobility."

Amanda thought about Clorisa and her father somehow feeling cheated by her friend. The one thought that towered above all was the fact that her maidservant was beyond reproach until today. This one small fragment of life was the only flaw she'd ever seen in her friend. And maybe that's why it stood out as much as it did. Amanda also knew how convincing and selfish her father could be. He would use a beautiful woman like Clorisa for his own ends. He would take advantage of her weakness. It was a way of life for him; he did it in his business every day. She would not be able to hold this one indiscretion against her friend. There must have been a good reason for what she did. So be it. A friend is a friend.

Amanda and Clorisa would leave immediately, riding south to the place of her birth. Sir Roth and Ellen would come along; business as usual her father would say. The funeral had passed but she would pay her respects. Amanda neither asked nor informed the duke about her trip. If he had said no she would have gone anyway and his spies would keep him up to date faster than she ever would.

Sir Roth no longer wore the Huxley crest and of that Amanda was glad. Any man wearing that crest would be less than welcome by the inhabitants of the farms and village where her escorts had raped the young woman last fall. Huxley made enemies north and south and used the King's gold to protect himself in the guise of serving the land.

Amanda could not keep her eyes from the knight ahead. She loved watching him; his every move a new adventure, his presence magical. She thanked the Gods for bringing him into her life and cursed the same Ones for her union with Huxley.

Snow still lay deep in the woods and across shaded parts of the trail. Chipmunks and squirrels scurried through the forest in search of food. Birds flittered through the barren trees doing the same. Racoons awoke from their dens testing the air as though in disbelief a new season had begun. The deer were fat this spring as food was plentiful, a mild winter it had been.

The day definitely did not drag on for Amanda; time flew whenever she was with her knight.

The sound of horses from behind put Sir Roth on guard. He ordered the soldiers to form a skirmish line before the women then drew his sword. Another knight at the head of a dozen men wearing the Huxley crest stopped before them.

"The duke ordered me to escort you to the grave of your father," said Beamish, Huxley's new first knight.

"There is no need as I have my own guard," said Amanda.

"It was an order to me and have no choice so I will follow."

Amanda knew they had been sent to spy on her. She would let them stay for the time being so said no more.

They rode with Huxley's troops not far behind. Amanda found all of Huxley's soldiers brash and loud in dire need of discipline. Her own troops remained quiet awaiting an order.

The chipmunk heard the horses coming and stuck his head out of rotted oak tree. He knew it was a dinner bell for him as one of the humans always left food around. Using stealth and courageous stalking techniques he would relieve them of some of their tastier treats.

It had been a warm winter but raids from bigger game than he had used up his food stores before spring. It seemed everything in the forest was bigger than he was. He'd worked hard all fall building the biggest supply yet. He'd made himself too big a target though. Rich chipmunks were always robbed.

So these humans riding their beasts came along just in time. He watched as they set up camp, cooked their watery foods, and ate. There were lots, two groups in fact wearing slightly different things. One group was noisy and these humans dropped lots of things on the ground.

The sun set and in the light of dusk the chipmunk scurried

to examine the morsels on the ground. He stopped in mid stride unable to believe. One of the flat disks they ate from sat on a log and had a wedge of food set upon it. There were walnuts on top and a cream underneath. Yum. What a find. He carried all the nuts back to his tree then returned for the rest. He ate the sweat bread that held the cream. He was full.

He sped to his tree and lay by the walnuts unable to eat another bite. He stared from a hole and saw one of the people who were different, not dressed like the rest, staring at the disk he'd just taken food from. She looked at it clearly upset. He would have to lay low; they would be looking for him. Belly full, soon he was asleep.

Night soon shrouded them, camp fires burning bright, warming the chilly air of early spring nights. Amanda, Clorisa, Ellen, and of course her knight, Sir Roth sat around the burning logs laughing and talking of the days events.

Amanda could feel Beamish's eyes upon her. He was here to spy and report every move she made, the duke hoping her to be unfaithful. He could drown her and the dowry would still be his. She would give him little to report as her voice was little more than whispered when she spoke. The unruly shouts and obnoxious laughs of his men would drown out whatever Amanda and the others had to say.

They soon arrived at the farm where her escorts had raped the young woman last fall. She knocked at the door bringing the farmer's wife, a smile upon her face when her eyes met Amanda's. When she noticed the soldiers, her eyes filled with fear.

"Do not worry, they are my troops. I stopped to inquire of your daughter as I hope she is well."

"She lives in fear as you would expect. You are not here to avenge the other soldiers?" said the farmer's wife.

"No, their fate was just. I apologize for their actions."

"Thank you but it was not your fault. My daughter will marry when a new cottage is built for the couple this summer. She has survived their assault. I thank you for helping her."

"I am glad all is well and good day to you."

They rode awhile then Amanda pulled her horse to the side of the road. Sir Roth noticed and rode to her side. Amanda counted Huxley's soldiers, twelve plus the knight.

"You have to keep and eye on Huxley's misfits, they are trouble," said Amanda.

"I know I was with them for a year. The duke likes them wild and unruly thinking them more dangerous that way," said Sir Roth.

That night Huxley's soldiers drank more than their ration of ale finishing all they had. They were asleep far ahead of the others. Amanda wanted to go to Damon, sneak over in the moonless night but the risk was too great. It was all Beamish would need to fuel the duke's final revenge.

Two days further south they came to a branch in the road. Amanda and the others continued south and Sir Roth rode east to the castle of the King. Amanda stopped and watched him disappear through the corner of one eye not wanting Beamish see her looking toward him directly. Amanda rode behind Huxley's soldiers making sure no one turned to pursue her knight. The duke and those under him were completely unpredictable. They lived by a code totally foreign to hers and answered to no God she was familiar with; they were ale hall brawlers in uniform.

They arrived at Dorville castle her Brother Andrew rushing

to greet her. They hugged and kissed as she released big sobs. Above all on her mind this moment was not her father's death but the duke's troops; Beamish watching her every move. She had no intentions of playing hide and seek with Huxley's fools.

"Andrew, before we go any further would you please lock up every man wearing the Huxley crest. We will talk about it later."

Beamish drew his sword followed by the others.

"Do you see why? They are dangerous idiots."

"Bring up the archers," yelled Andrew.

Rushing to the words of the newly appointed Duke twenty archers arrived along with fifty more men racing their way from distant barracks. Huxley's soldiers dropped their swords as though the steel burned their hands. They would spend their time in prison and be released upon return to Kara Keep.

CHAPTER XIII

With the duke's men behind bars Amanda was free to mourn her father in privacy and meet with her brother. Andrew was much like her father and six years older than her so they had little to do with each other over the years. He gave his time if she asked but never volunteered it. Asking him for anything seemed like an imposition so she rarely requested favours.

In church where her father lay entombed she prayed for his soul. Upon rising she saw the priest that had married her to the duke. She couldn't believe her eyes but there he was. What was he doing here?

"Andrew, look at that priest, the one by the railing. Do you know him?" said Amanda.

"He is the one who looked over our father after his death. He said it was heart failure."

"He is Duke Huxley's priest, the one who married us. They said he left at the beginning of winter."

Amanda saw the puzzled look on her brother's face as she had troubling thoughts of her own.

"In the marriage contract father signed what happens if father dies, and you die?"

"You become Duchess."

"Now what happens should I die with without an heir?"

"With an heir Huxley would become Duke until the heir

was of age. Without an heir he would still inherit your lands as there would not be a Daggot left for the title to revert to. Yes, I believe the King would give him ownership."

"Do you not see no matter what happens as long as the three of us are dead he gets everything."

"Is he that ruthless a man? Three dead, that is taking a big chance. The King would suspect something."

"The King would know something was wrong but without proof would not change the outcome. The duke would gamble on him doing nothing. When my father signed that contract he invited a wolf into a sheep pen."

"I will have the contract looked into."

"Jail that priest or dear brother I think you will die and I not long after. Also rid yourself of any servants you do not fully trust and certainly those hired in the last year. Let your food be touched by no one you would not trust with your life as that is what I believe it will cost."

With that her brother left to jail the priest and rid the premises of new servants. Amanda asked Clorisa and Ellen to arrange the transfer of sheep to the north. Andrew returned as she requested, more business needed to be tended today.

"I'm going to move the majority of our sheep north. The land there is hilly and rock filled good for little else other than grazing. We are wasting flat farming land here for grazing when we could grow grain instead."

"How many sheep will you move?"

"Eventually over a thousand but only five hundred this year as I think it a chore to move that many this summer. We will drive a hundred north at a time. I will need the protection of twenty of our soldiers with each move."

"They are yours and whatever else you need."

"That is it for now so let us dine. I haven't seen Mary in a year. When will you wed the woman? You have loved her for years."

"I would have long ago but she is barren and can never provide me with an heir. Actually I was waiting for you to have children so we could wed. If you provided lineage then the pressure would be off me to do likewise. I do not want our family line to end with us and neither does Mary. She will not wed me until your children can attend our wedding."

"She loves you too I think, thinking of you before her own happiness. As for me well I would rather not talk of that further. I will tell you a secret which you must share with no one. Promise?"

"I promise."

"I love another, a knight Sir Damon Roth. If the duke would let me go someday then it is him I would wed. I know Huxley will not let me go but I can dream can I not?"

"I am distressed to hear the type of man you have wed and want you to know that you are not alone in this. I will attend the King and ask for his help in resolution. I will think on the matter and we will come to some sort of arrangement. Maybe we can buy you out of this mess. It is my life as well that hangs in the balance. I know I have not been much of a brother to date but with father dead and us the last of the Daggots I feel closer to you than anyone save Mary. Do not give up hope whatever you do."

"I thank you for that dear brother and hope to someday have many children so that you can wed your love."

Amanda took her brother by the arm and walked him to the dinning hall where Mary was directing the staff.

Two days later while signing papers in the study Sir Roth

appeared carrying a leather case. She attacked him, grasped his cloak, kissed him and kicked the door shut. She locked it and drew the curtains. They made love on the bear rug near the hearth then lay in silence each hungry for the other.

"I attended the King and explained your plans to make Kara Keep self sufficient. I also explained you agreement with Rogun. I told him of the duke's objections to all you were intending to do," said Damon.

"What was his reaction?"

"He's given me letters, one for you. I'll get it. Here."

Amanda opened the letter breaking the King's seal. It detailed the changes he was making at Kara Keep. The duke would be allowed fifty soldiers and five knights as his private castle guards. He would have authority over the castle grounds only. The other three hundred and fifty soldiers would form the new frontier guard which would be headed by Sir Damon Roth. Amanda shrieked with excitement as her plan just took a giant leap toward reality. Both still nude they made love again Amanda hoping it would never end.

"I want to deliver this letter to him myself," said Amanda.

"He'll think you had something to do with it, no I'll take it to him. Remember I'm the new keeper of the peace. You mind yourself, you hear or I'll clasp you in irons."

Amanda said her good byes at the castle and rode beside Damon to Kara Keep. One hundred sheep walked before them, a dozen herding dogs keeping them in line. Twenty soldiers wearing the Daggot crest rode guard before and behind the lengthy procession. Beamish and the dozen men under him were now under the direct orders of Sir Roth as per declaration by the King. Sir Roth told them all that any man not silent would not ride but lead his horse until he learned to keep his mouth shut. Amanda knew he would turn this bunch into soldiers as good as any in the land.

Amanda rode beside her knight and Clorisa directly behind beamed with delight. Every time Amanda looked back at her the smile on Clorisa's face broadened as she nodded in approval. Ellen took her new position seriously riding back and forth overseeing all, missing nothing. She rode with a sick lamb draped in the saddle the ewe walking beside her horse looking up in concern at her sick child. All was as it should be thought Amanda; work was being done and all were happy in the doing. Love was all around in the hearts of people and animals alike.

Camp had to be made two hours before darkness set in. A grassy meadow suitable for grazing had to be picked and firewood gathered. Amanda and Clorisa cooked for all including the dogs. They worked well into the night cleaning up after the last soldiers had their fill. They'd brought a wagon this trip loaded with everything necessary to make stew. Soup and bread was all they would eat for the next ten days with almost forty people and a dozen dogs to feed.

Amanda wiped her brow and looked at the sleeping men. Clorisa was still cleaning the big iron pot used to make their stew. It took sometime before it cooled down enough to touch and was always last on the list of chores.

Amanda smiled as Ellen walked among the sheep on her toes lest she wake one. Tending animals was in her blood and her only passion. Ellen told her she would take the first watch but Amanda suspected she would be there longer than that. Directly behind her was Pepper one of the black and white

106

sheep dogs that had taken an instant liking to Ellen. All day long Pepper had one eye on the sheep, the other on her.

Amanda watched her knight as he tossed and turned in an unsettling sleep. She suspected that his wounds had not fully healed and maybe never would. She would asked Clorisa to slip some herbs into his food to help him sleep; the same kind she would take before the duke's love making to dull her senses.

They had been lucky on the way down as little rain came their way. It was still early spring and this morning was a reminder of that. Rain poured and doused the campfires making bread and salted beef their morning meal.

The rain was relentless as three days passed without campfires to cook or keep them warm through the damp, chilly nights. Many including Sir Roth coughed the day long. Everyone was sick of salted beef and bread so some chewed carrots instead.

Halfway through the fourth day of rain a miracle came their way, sunshine. Amanda ordered all to halt and told the soldiers to gather firewood. Although the logs were wet she used oil to aid in starting the fire. Sometime later all including the dogs had their fill of hot stew.

The remainder of their journey they stopped whenever the showers died. Once after halting the rains returned before the fire could be started then after abandoning a warm meal and starting their journey again, the rain stopped as though taunting them.

Horrible as the journey was it had to end and did exactly that. Amanda stared at Kara Keep wanting to turn around and go back. She wanted to ride side by side with her loving knight; return to Dorville and spend the rest of her days making babies with him. She dreaded the thought of even seeing the duke again; the thought of his touch make her skin crawl.

"You go in first so it won't look like we're doing this together. I think him to be in a foul mood after he reads his letter," said Sir Roth.

"I do not want to go in at all. I would rather stay at the inn," said Amanda.

"He'll come and drag you back. Appearances mean everything to him."

"I know dear knight, I will go. Later then."

CHAPTER XIV

Amanda rode into Kara Keep and handed Sapphire's reins to the stable boy. She walked into the front entrance of the castle and went immediately to the great hall. She wanted to get the formalities over with; wanted to hear his complaints and wishes of ill will then go to her room. The duke sat with Dione and did not acknowledge her in the least so she turned and walked away.

"Be in my chamber tonight," said Huxley.

Amanda heard Dione laughing and wanted to run, to stay at the inn but had no idea of what he might do. She had to keep reminding herself of the power that man had over her and all his subjects. He was the bearer of justice in this land and could kill whomever he wanted. The only thing keeping her alive was her dowry and her position in the Daggot clan. She'd underestimated him already as he was aiming for more than her dowry. He wanted all her lands including Andrew's fortune and had she not seen the priest he may have gotten it. Trying to lower herself to his level she could think of a lot of ways he could make her suffer. He could simply kill her horse or hang Clorisa for witchcraft. He was the law. No she would bide her time and try to stay one step ahead of him. She waited for Damon's letter that would demote him. He'd still rule the keep but not the lands beyond. Soon she would have somewhere to run.

Amanda changed and was on her way to see Agnes when the sound of shouting filled the castle. She knew Sir Roth had given him the letter. She rushed to the great hall where the duke stood sword in hand. Sir Roth backed away from him.

"It's my land and I won't let you steal it," said the duke.

"It's the King's land and he's taken it. You're lucky he left you the castle," said Sir Roth.

"Then get out now before I kill you."

"I am head of the frontier guard and have the right to be anywhere I desire and at this moment I'm telling you to pick the men you want. I give you that much. If you haven't picked the castle guard by tomorrow then I will do that for you but believe me you'll get the worst fifty men and five knights I can find."

"You and that bitch did this to me. Turned on me. I risked my life for yours and this is how you repay me. Get out."

Amanda left the hall as soon as Sir Roth did and couldn't stop the smile forming on her lips. She wanted to tell Huxley that she'd seen the priest and Andrew had jailed him. Huxley though would send another assassin in his place. Best to keep quiet and see what formed out of the king's changes.

That night the duke drank more than his fill and retired to his chamber early, Dione following him a smile on her lips, no shame in her heart. Amanda did not go to his chamber and as he had not sent for her so she went to bed.

The night not yet finished brought knocks upon their chamber door. It was Agnes in dire need of Clorisa. Amanda followed Agnes and Clorisa to the front hall where Dione lay looking like she was beaten to death.

"She's alive but just barely," said Clorisa.

Huxley appeared at the head of the stairs.

"Get that tramp out of here. Take her back to the inn where I got her from," he yelled.

"Can she be carried to the inn?" asked Amanda.

"It's too far, she might not make it," said Clorisa.

"We will take her to my room until she is better," said Amanda.

They started up the stairs toward Amanda's room Huxley scowled at them but said no more. Amanda had none but disgust for the man; he almost killed Dione because he'd had a bad day and because he could, so he did.

Amanda helped Clorisa tend to Dione. Her upper teeth had been broken off at the gum line and face bone broken. Her good looks would be forever lost as nothing would completely heal. She would be deformed for the rest of her days and all in the village would know the cost of lying with the duke. No wench would ever grace his bed of her own will.

Time passed slowly as she rarely saw her knight Sir Roth. She yearned for his touch and knew he felt the same way. She met with Melanie and told her Rogun would be welcome in the village. He could pick up twenty of the hundred sheep she'd promised and would hold him to his word on the truce.

Ellen came to her before leaving for Dorville to retrieve another hundred sheep.

"I think we can manage double what we did the last time. I talked to the sheep master and he agrees, at least two hundred he said maybe two hundred and fifty," said Ellen beaming with excitement.

"I put you in charge. Do what you think is right. That

is why I wanted you, you have a gift with animals," said Amanda.

"All right see you soon. Oh, and I love working with you Amanda."

That brought a smile to Amanda's face. Little things like that made life worthwhile.

The duke had been too drunk to pick the castle guard so Sir Roth did the choosing. He picked all the docile men and the elderly soldiers. Amanda was delighted with his choice as they were the men she would have selected, the ones she talked to. Huxley was almost on his own she thought yet still dangerous.

Next day she heard shouting from the great hall again and entered to see Sir Roth arguing with the duke.

"I fine you one hundred gold coins for what you did to Dione. The sum will be given to her as atonement for your act," said Sir Roth.

"I give you nothing. I'm the duke here you're nothing but a soldier so get out," said Huxley.

"Then I'll take the sum out of rents paid to you from the land you personally own."

The duke slid his sword from the table and attacked Sir Roth who parried the blow with his own. Huxley fought like a madman as Sir Roth had trouble keeping up using his left. He still hadn't mastered the use of that hand after his right was injured. Sir Roth's sword flew to the far end of the room as he fell on his back. The duke was about to thrust at him when Amanda stepped between them.

"If you do this I will go straight to the King and tell him of your actions. You are through Huxley; I have made peace with Rogun and also found your priest at Dorville. Andrew will not die and you go nowhere. My brother will also seek the King's help to have my marriage to you annulled. I think the priest will talk. Like I said you are through so put down that sword and save what little you have left. If you have the intelligence for that," said Amanda.

"I don't need you anyway you skinny bitch. I've enough money from rents to keep the castle going so yours will be the first throat I cut. I still have dominion inside this castle where my word and actions are law," said Huxley.

He turned his sword toward Amanda.

"You will not do that I swear," said Agnes standing with a butcher knife in her hand.

Agnes stood at the head of the kitchen staff all armed with some form of weapon. It was Clorisa who came up behind the duke while he stared at the others. Smooth and with the skill of an assassin she grabbed his chin from behind and sank a dagger into his back. She must have known exactly where to put it as the duke dropped without sound and lay motionless on the floor. Clorisa said she would kill him and did exactly that. What did she used to do before becoming her mother's servant so many years ago? Her maid would avoid the subject, she always had.

"Did you think we would let him kill you dear lady, we've been watching," said Agnes.

Sir Roth stood and retrieved his sword. He was silent for a time staring at the duke's body then spoke.

"I'll report to the King that thieves somehow gained access to the castle. He died bravely defending his wife and staff."

Amanda looked down on the Huxley's body not knowing what to think. He was dead, simple as that. It was over.

Amanda felt nothing at all but relief. She looked to her friends one and all.

"I've been blessed in this life to have so many good friends and thank you all. I owe you my life and will not forget that."

She ran to them and hugged them one by one. She hugged Clorisa and gazed into those hazel eyes. No words could ever be spoken that would do justice for her friendship. She said nothing but couldn't stop the tears.

"It's over Mandy," said Clorisa.

The funeral procession wound its way through the village. Huxley's body was placed in a grave at the base of the castle. Clorisa wanted him buried at the spot where they dropped the horse manure from the keep but Amanda objected. Few attended the funeral and those that did were there only for show; no one wept and all left as soon as the body landed in the grave. His loving wife attended, Sir Roth the official representative from the King, Clorisa, and Agnes.

Dione was now a member of the household staff, humbled by what had transpired. She obeyed Agnes and worked as hard as the others.

Amanda met Damon whenever she could which was often. The traditional mourning duration for a widow was half a year so she would wait that long before marrying the knight. They made love but took precautions as she wanted no illegitimate children.

Time passed and a wedding took place at the inn. Bridesmaids dressed in white surrounded Amanda as Clorisa gave the bride away. Flowers adorned the inn and cheers rang out after the groom kissed the bride. Amanda smiled at all as she stepped into the carriage drawn by white horses. Flowers filled the air before showering onto the carriage. They rode to the keep for their wedding night.

More than a thousand sheep had been moved to Kara Keep and a trade route in use. Rogun was a regular at the village inn and the pass north had been widened into a road.

That autumn when the leaves began to turn a surprise came to the villagers at the keep. Wagons rolled in stopping short of the hamlet and the occupants set up camp. Tents were erected, the grandest anyone had ever seen. In one, tables were set and goods of all kinds placed upon them. There were fine cloths in all colours and thread: there were tools, weapons, silverware, and more.

Amanda declared that a yearly fall fair would be had by all at Kara Keep. They were making money now so needed someplace to spend it she'd said.

The largest tent held a stage and benches inside where entertainers practiced their craft. There were singers and dancers: there were clowns, acrobats, and a man that made rabbits disappear.

Outside games of skill could be played for a price in hopes of winning a prize.

It was only to run for three days but the turnout demanded more time so was it lengthened to a week.

The wagons departed and soon after winter came their way; this one cold and savage but short.

A year passed and the cry of a child making its way into the world sounded throughout the castle. A messenger galloped toward Dorville with news of a baby boy, Edward, born to Amanda and Damon. Andrew and Mary could wed.

Two years later a cry loud enough to startle the guards on the ramparts of Kara Keep echoed throughout the castle. Morgana daughter to Amanda and Damon entered the world sending messengers south to announce her arrival.

PART TWO

MORGANA

CHAPTER XV

Youth and time pass quickly in this world, we never have enough of either in our lives. Morgana had those thoughts on this silent cold night. Eighteen years since her birth had passed in a heartbeat.

Morgana knelt on the ground three arrows stuck in the snow before her, one nocked and taut in her bow. She glanced at her father doing the same. The northern raiders were beaching their ship and moving inland, walking their way. The man in the lead wearing chain mail armour carried a large broad sword. He was Rolf a king among them. He was her target and if no other, that man must die today. The figures coming her way were engulfed in swirling whirlwinds of snow. It looked as though ghosts moved among the warriors choosing sides. These bearded men of the north dressed in leather and furs. With swords and shields at a distance they looked bigger than life.

Morgana glanced at her father, his bowstring still slack. The command that would bring his guard to attack was the arrow released from his bow. All the raiders save two guards followed the wary king. The raider was no more than thirty paces away and stopped. He stared into the brush hiding her as though he knew she was there. An arrow whistled through the air striking him in the chest. The arrow hung lifelessly from the chain mail.

Morgana fired hitting his face plate; the arrow splintered and the pieces were lost in the snow. Twenty-five of her father's northern guard attacked the raiders from the woods on both sides as she pulled back on the string of her bow. Her second arrow struck below his face plate and lodged in the right side of his throat. His warriors rallied around him as Morgana's third arrow pierced his right calf forcing him to his knees. Her father's arrows ended the lives of two men at the leader's side. Others took their place and dragged him back to the ship.

"Halt let them go," yelled Sir Damon Roth.

Ten killers running around the countryside was the worst situation they could have. That's why her father told all not to cut them off from their ship. Kill them or let them go was the order of the day.

Morgana fired every arrow in her quiver at the ship as the raiders rowed away from shore. Four hit their marks as men screamed; others stuck in the bow or the sail. The carved dragon head that led the raiders to this place stared stone faced toward shore during their retreat.

The northern raiders called themselves kings of the seas and as no one opposed them they were probably right. They wintered on small islands off the northern shore of this huge isle. They could appear on any shore at any time. They could sail deep into the heart of the country using the rivers in place of the seas.

The raider Rolf was particularly clever, taking much from this northern land. Her father came to this distant shore to help Rogun chief of the area tribes. Rolf's loot was not gold or silver as none here had those metals to steal. The raider's booty was the most precious of all, people. He took them and sold them as slaves. Morgana knew her arrow did not inflict a mortal wound. The one in the throat was to his right; in the centre or left and he would now be dead.

Morgana could never speak of her part in this battle, her mother would be furious at her father. She was already upset at Morgana, a young woman following the warrior ways of a knight. There was no way to explain to her mother about the call she heard but her father knew and understood. The blood of a warrior flowed through her veins and playing another role would only rob her of life. Her father had been taking her on most of his campaigns lately claiming they were hunting trips and nothing more.

Morgana had always felt the luckiest girl alive to have a knight as her father. She'd learned to ride at four with her mother and Ellen as teachers. At ten her father had taught her how to use a bow. She never abandoned her training and now at eighteen could shoot as well as his top archers. He'd taught her to be evasive in her moves; being small and light she would have to evade, not attack. She would have to rely on weapons that gave distance between herself and the enemy like the bow or at least a spear.

She had a short broad sword on her hip but her father discouraged its use. If she parried the sword thrust of a large man she would be swept away like a rabbit. She would have to rely on the extra distance of the bow. The sea raiders considered it a woman's weapon and seldom made use of it.

Morgana thought of her brother, exactly opposite to her. He had been her mother's son as much as she was her father's daughter. Edward had no lust for the sword and was the businessman of the family, outdoing both her mother and Uncle Andrew. He was south at Dorville arranging the purchase of more land as if they needed more.

Dawn made its way to them as they watched the ship sail and leave. The raiders would have the arrows out of Rolf by now and he would be drunk on mead for a week. One more shot was all she needed; she had the line, just one more shot.

Morgana wondered what damage was inflicted on the raiders when emptying her quiver of arrows toward the ship. It was not something her father would do; he fired only at sure targets. She would have to learn to control her emotions, learn how to loose.

It was all they could do for the present and would return to Kara Keep two days ride south. Morgana rode Trinket, granddaughter to Sapphire her mother's horse. The one she'd ridden to this land from her home in the south twenty years ago. Stories of her mother's arrival and the duke abounded; just pick one you wanted to believe. Neither mother nor father would talk about it, growing irritable if pushed on that subject. Morgana could feel there was a secret there and secret it would stay as far as she was concerned. Both parents had been honest and open with her about all else so if something had to be shielded then she would have to assume good intent.

That night all around the campfire were quiet as mice. Morgana would normally be the one to cheer the others but that was not the case today. Three comrades had given their lives and they had accomplished little with the sacrifice they made. The raiders they'd killed would be replaced as soon as they reached home port. She'd heard warriors stood in line waiting for room on one of those ships. Rolf would heal and they would be taking slaves in another week.

The end of the next day Kara Keep loomed on the horizon.

Her mother had made every attempt over the years to make the place look friendly but failed. The stones had all been washed down and sanded but still appeared a dull dark grey as the cliffs it sat upon, the stone that was used to make the keep. The shadows it cast made it black in places, an ominous sight regardless of what was done. It was built to frighten and succeeded in its designer's intent. Frightening it was.

They rode up the winding path to the northern gate which groaned and creaked open as it had always done. They entered the cobblestone courtyard their sounds echoing within the castle walls. Orders were shouted by the captain of the guards as Morgana dismounted and handed Trinkets reins to a stable boy. They were home again safe and sound within those dark walls.

Morgana walked through the castle door and into the front hall. Clorisa greeted her return with a smile and a hug. Coming from the great hall she heard her mother's loud voice so entered curious as to what the fuss was about. Her mother was not easily upset so it must be something of importance. She was talking to an emissary sent by the king a week ago, count Dabar.

"I will sign no contract that forces my daughter to wed. She will have a man of her own choosing," said Amanda.

"The king highly recommends this alliance as it will profit all," said count Dabar.

"It will not profit nor please my daughter to wed someone out of duty instead of love. She will pay a daily price for as long as she lives. We may even let a wolf into our lives to prey upon us. Believe me dear sir I know of what I speak. I will not sell my daughter to please the king," screamed Amanda.

Morgana was astounded by what was taking place. She'd

never seen her mother this way. When shouting at the count her mother moved his way as though an assault was her intent. She looked like an enraged animal ready to spring for his throat.

"May I suggest an alternative? Your daughter to visit, just visit mind you to see for herself," said the count.

Amanda's brow rose when she realized Morgana was in the room.

"What do you think Damon?" asked Amanda.

Morgana was startled to find her father not far behind.

"Our daughter will someday marry and now is as good a time as any that she look at eligible men. I am of the same mind as you; she will have a man of her choosing," said Damon.

"All right count Dabar. I will not object to my daughter travelling to the lands of which you speak, to visit," said Amanda.

"Neither will I. Know the final decision is still yours Morgana whether you stay or go," said Damon.

The count straightened and relaxed slightly, his composure returned.

"Well enough. We await your decision young lady. The Duke of the lands of which we speak has two strong sons your age. I could if you desire send word for them to travel here and court you among your own surroundings. I do however recommend you visit them so you can see your new home should you wed. I do not believe you will be disappointed in the land or the young men," said the count.

"It is quite a lot you lay at my feet. I will think on it but do not expect an answer for several days. I have friends to consult," said Morgana.

At dinner that evening no one even mentioned the

McBoden boys or her trip. Morgana knew her parents meant exactly what they said; in a matter as serious as this they would both speak from the heart. The first person she would speak to in the morning was Ellen; a beautiful woman whom had never wed. Morgana wanted to know her reasons and if she felt the same way then maybe would never wed either. Second and most important was to speak to Clorisa and hope she could get the old woman to open up to her. Being in a similar position as her mother she had to know more about her, the duke, and what drove her mother here in the first place.

Morgana couldn't sleep that night and doubted she ever would; people were turning her life upside down. Why couldn't they just leave her alone and let her find her own way through life? What did she owe the king anyway? He had no right to order her into a lifetime of strife and sorrow; it would be like sending a knight into eternal battle. She tossed and turned more frustrated than sleepy so finally gave up her bed and dressed. She made her way to the kitchen for tea and found Clorisa at the table crying.

"What is wrong Clorisa?" asked Morgana.

"It's going to happen all over again and I'm too old to go along and help," said Clorisa with a sob.

"What is going to happen again? Please tell me. I need to know."

"The king is going to force your parents to sign a marriage contract and you'll be with some madman till he kills you."

"What? Is that what happened to mother?"

"Yes. The duke would have taken her life but we took his first, me and Agnes and the staff."

"I do not think my parents will bow to the king in a matter such as this. Did my grandfather force mother to go?"

"Yes but she also went out of a sense of duty to king and country. Pride and self sacrifice was what made her journey here in the beginning."

Morgana hugged Clorisa then talked the duration of the night. The topic changed when the kitchen staff arrived at sunup. Morgana eyed one and all after discovering what had taken place twenty years before. Agnes had passed away last winter but other than that they were still all here. She hoped that during her life she would make friends such as these.

Ellen rode her new horse Flashfire to the sheep farm and was intercepted by Morgana. They talked of events that had taken place since their last meeting. Morgana told Ellen of her part in the attack on the raider. She could talk to her about things like that knowing secrets were safe with her friend.

"Mother must never know," said Morgana.

"Your mother was just as reckless as you when she was young. Ask her about the scar on her shoulder," said Ellen.

"What did she do?"

"Rode through an enemy line to get help. The scar she got from a arrow wound. She almost died of infection and would have had it not been for the Clorisa and her magic with herbs."

"And she scorns me for wearing a sword?"

"She worries."

"Tell me truly why you never married."

"I like animals more than men. No that's not the reason. Could you see me pregnant and depended on a man? I'm too wild for that."

Morgana had discovered more about her mother in the last day than all of her life. She was in a similar position and her friends must have felt they owed her as much as they could give.

Her parents had tried to make her feel as though she wasn't pressured but she was when the king sends emissaries to strike a bargain with her as the prize. Amanda had honoured the king's request out of duty. Morgana would also but out of a sense of adventure, take a look in any case. She'd never been away from home but now smiled to herself as excitement rose. Morgana had a lust for it as she did for battle. After all, they told her she had no obligations, just visit.

"I'm going to take the trip," said Morgana to her parents.

"Pick the men you want for and escort," said her father.

"You know who I'll pick for captain, Bluko. Are you sure you can spare him that long?"

"For you, anything."

"It is almost spring. I'll leave at first thaw."

CHAPTER XVI

Two weeks later Morgana rode Trinket south behind the captain of her escort, Bluko. Beside her was her handmaiden Malisa trained in the ways of healing and herbs by Clorisa. Morgana saw Malisa as chatty and soft but intelligent. She let Bluko hand pick the men forming her escort and the mounts they rode. He was a meticulous man in part responsible for her training and prowess with certain weapons. Morgana liked him, stubborn and hard yet caring in his own way.

Only three days south Morgana reached a point she'd never been. The soldiers from Barkley castle to the south patrolled north to this point. They would ride south to Dorville to see Andrew and Edward then west to Welton Castle in Morland. The people to the west had been in near isolation until recently as a road now linked them to the rest of the kingdom.

A forest stretching a length that required a four day ride to cross had separated east from west. A section the width of two wagons had been cut through the old growth. Before the road had been built the only way to Morland had been along the coast a ten day ride south.

The soldiers rode unopposed and were greeted by everyone they met being seen as keepers of the peace. The old Huxley crest that the people had feared and hated was laid to rest with the duke. Amanda had made immediate changes to soften the mood. In the village at Kara Keep she'd built a great hall for worship, meetings, and a place where people could go if seeking work. She'd sent emissaries along the roads giving tokens of friendship trying to undo the harm the duke and his soldiers had done.

The nights were cold in early spring making a campfire a necessity. The days grew longer and warmer Morgana needed only a sweater at times. It was still too early for animals to leave their dens in masses. A few hardy squirrels and chipmunks did brave the weather in search of food. Morgana set out early in the year so she would have sufficient time to travel and visit without ever having to rush.

The chipmunk heard the beasts trudging through the mud. He peeked at them from the shadows of his hiding place in the old rotted oak. His grandfather had been the first to see them discovering these humans were a source of food. And he needed something to eat, he was starving to death.

It had been a long winter and his nut stores were drained. To make matters worse one of his hiding spots had been raided by a big red squirrel, one third of his winter supplies stolen. He had been forced to come out of his den early this year in search of something to eat.

The humans made a fire and cooked watery things. But that, according to his father and grandfather before him, was not what he was looking for. He had to wait to see what they dropped on the ground then raid them in twilight and steal whatever he could. He'd been trained by his father to do just that.

They were eating and it looked like they were throwing food away. Were they setting a trap? There was always that possibility. Maybe they were sick of being robbed all these years and came to exact vengeance on him for what his family had taken in the past. Stealth would be the word of the day. They couldn't catch what they couldn't see.

Twilight came and he was ready. He slowly stalked, crawling on his belly toward the biggest piece he'd seen them throw away. He memorized all the places where they'd dropped or thrown morsels and crumbs. They sat around their fire totally unaware he was closing in on them. They would be easy prey. The biggest piece lay before him, it was crunchy bread. What more could he ask for?

He finished raiding them; they didn't even notice he was there. It was not an easy feat. It took years of training, cunning, and stealth to accomplish what he'd just done. They'd have to work a lot harder to catch him.

Sleep came easy that night, his belly exploding. In the morning he was awaked by their noise. He'd wanted to sleep in. They left and he rushed out for more of their scraps. It must be nice to have more than you can eat.

Morgana was both anxious and frightened to meet her suitors; anxious because a meeting with someone who could become the love of her life excited her; frightened because the wrong man could harm both her and her family. Morgana knew she did not have strength to endure what her mother had.

She was certain that if a man savagely beat her she would kill him regardless of outcome. He would be dead before he could get a second blow in. And maybe being able to defending herself is why her father pushed her hard as he did.

Morgana's hand maiden Malisa rode mostly in silence

looking about and enjoying the view. If questioned however she would burst out with an avalanche of words all strung together in a long chain.

"You look cold?" asked Morgana.

"Well no not really but sometimes, yes I am, but not right now, probably tonight I will be again, but don't think I'm complaining. What about you, are you cold?" said Malisa.

"No," said Morgana.

The castle gates at Dorville were open when they arrived. Edward had told her they opened at sunrise and closed after sunset. It was a place of business more than anything else. Before she could hand Trinket's reins to a stable boy Edward was upon her, hugging, lifting her from the ground, and spinning her round. He had done that since she was young and she had always loved him for it.

"Good day dear Brother," said Morgana.

"Welcome little sister. How long will you be staying with us?" asked Edward.

"Oh not long. Do you know why I journey south?"

"Yes, and next you will travel west. A messenger came to us a week ago."

"You have got a silly smile on your face. I am just going for a visit. I shall not wed without a lot of thought and a trip home for advice. What do you know of them?"

"They are a rich family in farming like us. That is probably why the king thinks it a good match."

"No, No, I mean the men I am to see, are they tall, fat or what?"

"I know, I was just getting to that, let me finish it all. It may take me a second or two to remember things."

"What? Have you met them?"

"Yes, I am making business arrangements with them regarding trading of goods. Now let me finish."

"All right."

"The oldest is Brent, tall, thin, but strong. Quiet man but quite brilliant actually. I will not get the better of him in business."

"How old?"

"Oh, you test my patience little sister. He is twenty-two, four years your senior."

"And the other?"

"I will not tell you of him as you keep interrupting. Now go and clean up and get changed. Dinner will be ready shortly."

And with that Edward gave her a spank on the bottom which she quickly returned.

At dinner uncle Andrew gave a toast in honour of the upcoming bride causing Morgana to throw a potato his way. Too much wine was had by all and the after dinner conversations were filled with too much laughter.

"Now tell me of the other one," said Morgana.

"What other one?" asked Edward.

"McBoden, the youngest."

"Oh, she is a girl of fourteen."

"No silly the man, the second oldest then."

"That is Gavin, twenty-years old, sandy brown hair, taller than you but shorter than Brent."

"What colour are his eyes?"

"I do not know, I never thought to ask. I did not see much of him. He was always in bed with the maids."

"What, with whom?"

"Jesting my dear, but not really, He is a ladies man alright, friendly, soft spoken and not at all shy but not forward either.

He has a distinctive charm about him; I do not really know how to put it. You will like him from the moment you meet him, all women seem to in any case. He is not as sly as Brent but really quite socially inclined."

"I cannot wait. What of the parents?"

"Absorbed in the running of the farms. They will not even know you are there."

"What else?"

"It is a poor land filled with poor people. Only a few families hold the wealth of Morland. It is not like anything you are used to. No knight has ever graced their land. It does not have mother's touch as Kara Keep. That is the greatest difference you will find, the lack of a woman's touch, no charity, little patience with the lower class."

"Maybe that is what I am sent there to change."

"Oh, do not even try to change that lot; they will fight your every step. They are proud people, even the lower class may be too proud to accept help especially from a stranger."

"Mother did it."

"All had a common cause and that was to rid themselves of the duke. Kara Keep was built by people with a common goal. It sprang to life due to the death of a man and stays united silently celebrating his demise. There is no such evil in Morland, only people comfortable with their station in life even be they penniless."

The night came to an end; Morgana was content to know at least something of the land and people to where she was going. She came here not only to visit but to seek her brother's advice. He had an uncanny ability to search out people's thoughts and their souls. Morgana had gotten more than she'd asked for today, Brent was his rival and Gavin was his opposite.

Sleep came to her quickly that night although her mind spun with questions about the men she would soon meet.

She spent a few more days visiting then wanderlust finally got the better of her and she left.

Morgana and her procession left the castle on the only road west. The land's of the south were flat and fertile, the soil rich and black. The kingdom's wealth was centered here, the lands west and north barely paying their way. Her mother had made Kara Keep self sufficient and was extending her influence to the lands around it. Morgana wondered if she was as capable as her mother but knew deep inside she was not like her and Edward. She was like her father and would have to remember that; don't try to be what you are not.

Morgana and party reached the old woods they said had been there since the beginning of time. The growth tall and dense flanked the road on both sides. Folklore told of creatures not of this world who travelled within, demons and ghosts of another time. They could be heard but were never seen, only shadows were ever witnessed. But everyone knew they were there waiting for someone to make a mistake. That thought sank feelings of dread into her heart.

Morgana's hair stood on end as she scanned the forest to either side. There was a stench in the air not familiar to her, the odour of something long since dead. Numerous stories of men missing or dead had been told when the road was being built. Rumours of travellers disappearing from sight abounded at inns near the start of the old wood. She felt like a trespasser here not part of this world. Morgana crinkled her nose at the thought of four days travel through this forest. She was never one to let old wives tales stop her from doing what had to be done. Her sword would deal with demons the same as anything or anyone else.

They came to an area cleared for camping at the side of the road. That first night Morgana slept little as sounds of night creatures rooting through the bush woke her often. Could the old wives tales be right? Icy fingers ran down her spine at that thought.

CHAPTER XVII

The next morning all were greeted by rain. The storm swelled like a dark wall, a solid front of billowing dark clouds coming their way. The packed roads were slick making caution the word of the day. Time dragged on as numbness set into the outer reaches of Morgana's body. Every part of her was soaked in frigid water making her hands and feet ice cold. She dismounted and led Trinket trying to warm herself but it was to no avail. That night a campfire could not be started so all sat and shivered unable to sleep. Morgana sat on a log hugging Malisa using each other's body heat to stay warm. It worked where they touched but her back and far side was frozen.

Malisa turned her head and softly spoke, "People die of cold like this you know. I've seen a man sitting like us frozen stiff. They had to break all his bones to straighten him out and bury him. Parts of him shattered like glass. They had to shovel those pieces into his grave. Can you imagine being scooped into a hole?"

"No I cannot Malisa. I have never actually thought about it."

Morning brought with it an end to the rain. The rays of the sun were like a reprieve from the Gods. The road ran east and west so the sun shone on them only twice per day, when it rose in the east and set in the west. But that was better than the day before. The rest of the day they rode in the shadow of the great forest. Whether right or left few rays penetrated the tall, dense bush.

Fresh water was not difficult to locate as streams were in abundance spanned by newly made wooden bridges where they crossed the road. Game was also plentiful as deer darted from the bush running from the unknown riders. Hunting was not required as the soldiers led four pack horses loaded with provisions and Morgana's possessions.

Morgana became bored with the pace so rode ahead then around a bend. There were bodies lying on the road. Her father's training had taught her caution when dealing with the unusual, it could be a trap. Highwaymen may lay in wait while their companions lay mocking death. Most travellers would rush to help only to be robbed and possibly become corpses themselves. She scanned the forest on both sides and strained for abnormal sounds. Captain Bluko came from behind and she signalled caution as he approached. Bluko signalled the soldiers behind to halt then slowly approached her overlooking the scene himself.

"I'm going to guard the rear. I'll send two men to advance. Back them with your bow," said Bluko.

"Yes sir."

Morgana was already stringing her bow and nocking an arrow when two soldiers rode by and slowly advanced. Ten more moved behind her then stopped.

With blood curdling screams northern raiders charged from the bush. The two men returned at a gallop, the raiders not far behind. She'd heard more screams from the rear and knew the attack came at both ends.

After the two scouts rode by and out of harms way she

and five archers fired on the advancing raiders. Four fell to the ground before reaching them but ten or more were almost upon them.

The mounted soldiers were outnumber but fought against warriors on foot and were able to hold their own. Morgana dropped back to use her bow but was afraid of missing a target and hitting one of her own so advanced again. She could hear the clanging of iron and shouts of men to the rear and knew help would not arrive from there anytime soon. She rode to within five paces of her next target and fired an arrow into a man's face as he raised his head to swing at her.

Morgana used her bow to push back a warrior and had it ripped from her grasp. She quickly drew her sword and drove it down into his chest. The sword stuck on bones and his backward momentum pulled her off Trinket. She managed to free her sword from the dead man's body and as she did found herself face to face with a man three times her size. She had bounced three arrows off the man's armour only a short time ago and now stood before him with her short sword in defence.

This was the type of fight her father had trained her to avoid but here she was opposing a man holding a weapon as long as she was tall. He grinned as his two handed broad sword swung down upon her. Her father's lessons ran through her mind as she leapt backward refusing to parry. Morgana ran and danced around him avoiding contact. She dodged and rolled to keep out of his reach.

Then as though the Gods had decreed she should live Bluko stood between her and the man. It wasn't easy for the captain; the man was huge and strong as a bull. She rushed to retrieve her bow nocking an arrow quick as she could. She had to help Bluko. Bluko ducked the big man's swing. At that second when the big man was exposed she fired an arrow into his throat from only ten paces away. He wavered and fell dead on the ground. Without a word both rejoined the battle.

Morgana nocked an arrow and fired into the calf of another warrior causing him to limp away. Her next arrow found the thigh of another. Morgana had kept her aim low so as not to hit one of her own in a vital area should she miss. At the sound of a horn the remaining raiders broke off the attack and ran.

Four of seven of their soldiers with her were still alive. One was badly wounded. The ones that could ran to aid soldiers at the rear but the raiders there had also run.

"What are sea raiders doing so far inland?" asked Morgana.

"The pickings on this road must be good," said Bluko.

Six of their soldiers had died and three were severely wounded. They buried the dead, Morgana taking her turn with one of their three shovels.

Malisa treated the wounded chattering aimlessly as she did. Morgana was surprised at her knowledge and skill. From the midst of the battle she'd heard that Malisa had pulled an injured man from danger. Without panic she tended the wounded mumbling strange chants to herself. They also told of her courage when a warrior raised his sword to cut her down. She stood bravely staring into the man's eyes and he backed away. Was it magic, they asked each other? No one knew.

The next day they left the forest behind and rode into open fields dotted with farms. The area was wet and humid, a light mist hung in the air. At first Morgana thought they were ponds then seeing so many knew they were bogs. The land looked rich and fertile but water was everywhere causing the road to twist and turn around swamps. They passed close to a farm where children waved as parents rushed them inside. Strange soldiers were never good news to peasants and usually associated with either war or tax collection.

The flat lands of the moors sat under a heavy bleak sky, the distant horizon hidden by fog. A gentle breeze refused to clear the air. The silent shroud of mist hung like and oppressive weight all around. From the hills to this wet level terrain was a greater change than she'd ever wanted to endure. The sea was the only thing worse. The few trees she saw looked knarred and deformed. The lifeless bogs that dotted the land lay like a threat. A few small shrubs grew here and there, homes for some small birds that fluttered about. Morgana was not impressed with the land and hoped for salvation in the men she was here to see.

That evening they came upon a small village large enough to accommodate an inn. The captain went inside and when he returned told them that food and lodging were available to the ladies. That was something afforded her above the others but she took it without any feeling of guilt. The two were women, after all, have special needs. She also had to do something with herself as she would be meeting two suitors soon. Morgana was relieved to learn she would have a warm meal and would sleep in a bed tonight. She had a feast fit for a king and devoured it without shame. Sitting at the table over her empty plate Morgana awaited the barkeeps return.

"How far to Welton castle?" asked Morgana.

"Half a day west."

So they would be there tomorrow about midday. Morgana had not forgotten about the two McBoden men, her purpose for being here.

"Do you have many problems with sea raiders in this area?" asked Morgana.

"Oh yes, once a year at least they come for valuables and to take slaves. We do our best and so do the McBodens but we never know where and when they're going to come," said the barkeep.

"We encountered them on the road a day east of here. Have they ever been spotted there before?" asked Morgana.

"Yes, we think they have a path from the sea through the old wood."

So that explained their presence; it was just ill luck on their part to run into them. Also ill luck for the raiders as it had cost them dearly and got nothing in return.

Morgana was able to take a bath and Malisa combed the knots out of her hair. She stopped at that as wearing scents was definitely not her way. In battle on a crisp day a woman's scent could be picked up downwind a good distance away. And that after all is what she lived for, battle, not silk or perfume.

That night sleep should have engulfed Morgana but it did not. She had those damn men on her mind again and couldn't get them out. The thought of them, the mystery made her toss and turn and sleep impossible. And what was so important about these two, there were thousands of eligible men around. It was just the fact that the king had narrowed her selection somewhat. And what if she defied him and chose one of his enemies. She shuddered at the thought. She would have to handle the king with diplomacy one way or another.

The next morning Morgana was already dressed as everyone woke. She sat at a table in the inn waiting for the barkeep to rise. She ate only bread and drank some tea, Malisa joining her beaming with a smile as usual. She would be underway this very moment but knew the soldiers needed time to load the pack horses. Morgana would not ride into the castle without an escort. It would make her look eager and that was not the image she wanted to portray. She wanted to be seen as a visitor and nothing more.

Normally when a woman met suitors they did so in a dress. If she took the time to do so it would mean unpacking her things: bathing again, washing her hair, dressing, then repacking, then loading the pack horse again. She was after all here only as a guest and dressed in her riding clothes could be taken for nothing more. She wanted a casual meeting and if necessary a hasty retreat.

Morgana no longer focused on the McBoden men. She scanned the countryside trying to get a feel for the land. Gently rolling hills made up the bulk of the scenery and water the rest. Few trees grew here making her wonder if that was natural or had the land been so well cleared. Few farm houses could be seen and the emptiness filled her with dread. She was used to the rough lands of the north, the tall trees, mountains, and rocks. Land with character her father would say, her mentor, her friend, and companion. She missed him already, the training, fighting, and hunting they did. She could go over it a hundred times and would still come to the same conclusion. She didn't like the lay of the land no matter how many times she went over it.

CHAPTER XVIII

Then finally there it was, set atop a hill, Welton castle. Another reason to run. At first sight she was disappointed to say the least and closing on it liked it less and less. It sat in a huge open space with walls built of various coloured stone and rock. It appeared as though materials to build it had been leftovers from other work. It looked patched together and overly repaired. There were towers at each corner but all were of different height. It looked like one big ugly mass of rock in the middle of a sea of green. Rubble built at different times with varying intent lacking even a hint of architecture.

Morgana stopped Trinket before a patched old gate and waited for it to open. She had seen no soldiers on the ramparts and heard not a sound. Someone surely must have seen them coming through the vast fields and along the road. She looked at Bluko who raised his eyebrows then dismounted. He walked to the gate and banged on it with the hilt of his sword. The sound of feet moving on the other side accompanied by Bluko's disapproving smirk.

The gates creaked, groaned, and snapped open. Two shabbily dressed soldiers holding broadswords stood with questioning looks but said nothing. Morgana wondered what they would do if thirty raiders were here instead of them. She shot a glance Bluko's way and saw the captain shaking his head at the sight. Morgana hoped she was at the wrong castle.

"Morgana Roth is my name. I believe I am expected."

"I'll get the captain," said one of the soldiers.

The man returned and following him was and entourage consisting of what looked to be every soul in this place. People streamed out of the castle, ladies, servants, men in uniform and without. All coming their way like a mob. Unfortunately she was in the right castle. A quick glance to the buildings inside revealed that they looked worse than the outer walls she had seen.

"Welcome Lady Roth, I'm Kevin McBoden."

"Good day sir," said Morgana.

"Please come this way," said Kevin.

So this was Duke McBoden the father of the men she was here to see. He was dressed as a farmer and not in the least like a man of nobility. Only here would anyone believe he was anything other than a peasant. She took full meaning to what her brother had said. He'd warned her that the people were poor and would find nothing here she was used to.

They followed the Duke to the stables, had their mounts tended to, and then were escorted inside.

"We're having our noon meal if you like to freshen up and join us," said the Duke.

Morgana looked in the mirror and saw a woman who'd spent a half day on horseback since her last bath. She fussed with her hair then washed her hands and face. It would take the better part of a day to make herself look fully presentable. She shook her head remembering it was only a visit so joined them at the table.

"This is my wife Martha and that's my son Brent, Gavin is not here at the moment," said the Duke.

Brent stood then walked toward her, bowed, then gently kissed her hand. He was a tall, gangly man, his hands seemed overly large, and his face narrow. His brown hair and brown eyes suited the rest of him, plain and without spark. Edward had described him as intelligent and she saw a cunning look in his eyes. Maybe not cunning though she thought, somewhat a longing look, yes a longing gaze directed at her. She didn't like it whatever it was; made her feel uncomfortable as though being appraised for an evening in bed. There was definitely nothing about him that she would ride a week to claim. She nodded to acknowledge him and he returned to his seat.

She'd almost finished her meal when two hands clasped her shoulders.

"This must be Lady Morgana, I'm Gavin dear lady, come stand, let's have a look at you."

Morgana stood and turned looking into the bluest eyes she had ever seen. She was unable to break her stare held by his spell.

"My but you're a lovely lady. Your brother Edward described you as a warrior, told us you fought beside your father, a knight. We expected a big woman with an axe in hand," said Gavin.

"I am sorry to disappoint you," said Morgana.

"That you have not done. I'm delighted with what I see before me, a warrior and a lady in one. A rare discovery."

His words took her eyes to his mouth, then his face, and then his hair. He was the most stunningly handsome man she'd ever seen. She saw nothing in his father or mother that would yield an offspring like him. Morgana suddenly realized that she was in fact staring; looking at him like he was a prize bull at a fair. She cringed and looked away hoping no one had noticed.

"I am delighted to meet you as well," said Morgana.

"After the meal would you join me for a stroll? I'll show you around," said Gavin.

"Yes, I would like that."

Everyone resumed their meal and Morgana shot glances at all. Brent sat with an intense look on his face, the look of a man defeated and not liking it. That was something she couldn't stand, a man who would give up before a battle had even begun. She was being harsh on him and knew it but as a warrior couldn't tolerate a quitter and that's what she saw.

Gavin on the other hand caught her eye from the start. She would give a man such as him much leeway, if she'd ridden the week and fought raiders to be with him today she would do it all over again in a flash. Gavin was a dream. Edward had told her she would like him from the start. He was brash, forward, and presumptuous but that only added to his charm. Gavin would handle anything she could throw his way so didn't even try to outwit him. This man would never give up in a fight or even falter.

Gavin made no attempt to show her the castle told her it was boring and old. He took her to the village, to a place where a merchant sold candy he said was second to none, home made by his wife. He took her to a quiet brook where they ate too many sweets and talked of nothing in particular, yet everything under the sun. He didn't try to mate her as others had, only wanted to know her favourite colour, her favourite food, her favourite everything. He made her feel important, somehow of more value than she'd ever felt before. He made her feel her opinion worth a king's ransom and her thoughts worth gold. Being with him was heaven on earth. She'd found her place in life, found beauty everywhere she had first felt disdain.

Morgana loved Gavin's touch and loved touching him. Looking into those blue eyes and hearing that soothing voice put her under his spell. She could not completely surrender to him this first day and he didn't ask. He was a gentleman in every way returning her to the castle well before sundown for the evening meal.

Had Morgana come to choose a suitor Malisa would accompany her wherever she went. In her letter she'd stated that her trip was a visit to business partners of her family. A real lady would never ride off with a man known only to her by the sitting of one meal but then she never claimed to be a lady. She was part warrior riding beside her father and camping with soldiers at night. If her virtue was in question let no one utter it to her out loud, and who cared what they thought. Rumours would abound no matter what she did.

At the evening meal she spoke freely not wishing to offend but wanting it known her opinions had voice. She told them of her first approach earlier that day and wondered if they knew how weak their defences were. Thirty raiders could have knocked upon the castle gate and two soldiers would have granted them entrance.

"Raiders don't come this far inland," said the Duke.

"They are coming further every year and in greater numbers. A group attacked us on the road here. They are taking slaves only half a day south of this castle," said Morgana.

"I was unaware of that. We're not soldiers dear lady, only

farmers. There isn't one real soldier among us. If you have advice we'll listen," said Kevin the Duke.

"They are not only raiders now in the east. They seek conquest. They may look for more here soon. You will need to set up defences. If they find out how weak you are, they will attack and believe me they will conquer," said Morgana.

"My son Gavin has been pushing me to do something so I put him in charge of it. Please help him wherever you can. I support you both in this matter," said Kevin.

"I will do what I am able. I will put Captain Bluko at your disposal. He is the one you need."

"And I appreciate your help and look forward to your company," said Gavin.

Morgana smiled at Gavin then nodded in approval. She glanced at Brent who had a depressing look about him. He looked truly unhappy and hoped it had nothing to do with her as she had no interest in him whatsoever.

Morgana retired early and fell asleep as soon as she climbed into bed, dreaming of Gavin the night long.

CHAPTER XIX

Morgana awoke at sunrise bathed and dressed for the day. It was a quick bath unlike the ones the ladies take. No oils or perfumes would touch her skin. The last thing she'd done the night before was talk to Gavin and arrange a drill with the soldiers this morning. She rolled her long hair into a bun and tied it with a leather cord. She slipped into her fighting leather garments and put on her chain mail vest. Morgana strapped on her sword belt then slid the sword in its sheath then did likewise with the dagger. She slipped a thin double edged knife into her right boot and another into the left then threw her gloves into her helmet and left the castle.

Gavin was already assembling the troops. Bluko sat on the deck steps shaking his head. Morgana walked past giving him an acknowledging tap on the shoulder.

"I think I'd better get started. There is a lot of work to be done here," said Bluko.

"You are probably right. They need something to spur them on."

Morgana looked at the soldiers standing in a ragged line, no two dressed alike. She smiled as Bluko approached knowing what the men were in for.

"Permission to take command," said Bluko to Gavin.

With a surprised look on his face he answered, "Well yes, please."

Morgana watched as Bluko walked toward the group and when he approached quickly drew his sword. The closest two men jumped back a step out of fright. He etched a long line in the dirt with the point of his weapon.

"Line up, toes on this line."

They lined almost tripping over each other.

"The worst dressed soldier of the day, every day get's to do battle with me. You, yes you, you're it for today.

Bluko put on his helmet and flipped the face shield down. The man he pointed to drew his broadsword, a smile pasted on the man's face. The soldier lunged forward and swung, Bluko ducking the blow. The soldier swung downward at Bluko who stepped to one side of his weapon. The sword smashed into the dirt and just as it did Bluko kicked the soldier's hand at the hilt causing him to drop the weapon. Bluko stood between the soldier and his sword slapping him with the broad surface of his blade. The soldier turned to run and Bluko slapped his butt with the flat surface again causing all to laugh.

Rushing to the line and standing at the end was Brent.

"You don't need to be here Brent, it's only for soldiers," said Bluko.

"Gavin and I are the commanders," said Brent.

"I wasn't aware of that. I'll run you all through some drills and show you how to guard a castle," said Bluko.

Captain Bluko yelled at the group calling them a disgrace to a uniform. Morgana laughed as she had seen him run his routine countless times before. She knew they were in the right hands but had some bitter medicine to swallow for some time to come.

Morgana asked Gavin to take her to the coast as arrangements would have to be made to set up a series of signal fires. These fires would alert the soldiers of an attack. That was the problem now as no one knew where and when the raiders would come. With signal fires the soldiers would know not only when but where the attack was coming from.

"We will get fishermen and farmers to build fires in a line not too far apart from coast to castle. When we see them we will send troops," said Morgana.

"How do we know a signal fire from another?" asked Gavin.

"The sender will use a blanket to hide the fire for a second then show it again three times, a simple code repeated over and over."

"What if they won't do it?"

"It is for their protection as well as ours. If they refuse or are lazy about it then just double tax them. You need it and they have no choice."

They arrived at one of several landing sites which would take raiders to the roads and villages beyond. They spoke with fishermen overjoyed with the idea. Everyone knew someone that had been taken as a slave. They stopped at farms and were offered food and assurances of help.

For a week they rode south everyday then west as well setting up a series of signal fire locations that ran like spokes of a wheel from castle to villages. If raiders landed on any southern or western shore then a signal fire would be started. Farmers were on constant vigil day and night and upon spotting a fire would start their own. During the day oil or simply water could be thrown on the wood to make it smoke. The next in line would start his until one within view of the castle was lit.

Soldiers would be dispatched following the fires south to their destination. It would take less than half a day for them to arrive at the coast. Raiders moving inland would be met by force in half that time. A few defeats in their community and word would spread that Morland was not the place to raid.

Morgana knew the main requirement at this time was a trained force to send against invaders. On the morning of the ninth day of her arrival she wanted to see what Bluko had accomplished. Today they were all in a straight line and neatly dressed.

"I'm having a hard time telling who the worst dressed is so I'll forget about it and jump to swordsmanship. Break into pairs and show me your thrusts and parries," yelled Bluko.

Morgana was amazed at the difference in only a week.

"Bluko you worked miracles again. Thank you."

"It's just a little polish. Some weren't too bad and only needed a little balance. Keep and eye on Brent. He's a natural. Good enough to be a knight someday if he has the courage," said Bluko.

"He has the reach alright and has more grace with a sword than in his walk but I think lacks bravery."

Morgana didn't know what to make of the man and his hidden talents. Intelligence equal to his own so her brother had said and now a sword hand that with training and practice would be equal to her father's. His look would attract no maiden including herself but there were things within him yet to be discovered.

That night at the dinner table Brent was as usual glum and looking defeated. Not the same man she saw at the sword practice in the afternoon. He was definitely not a social person and looked uncomfortable in the company of others. Gavin was beaming, his smile stretching his face out of shape. After dinner he walked to her side of the table and knelt beside her.

"Would you grace whatever life is left to me with your companionship? Would you give your hand to me in marriage?"

Morgana was shocked, her mind spinning, her heart full of joy. Was she still just a visitor? In absence of a knight she felt like a protector to this land. She had a place, purpose, and someone to love.

"Yes."

Morgana thought about her wedding: the location, her parents, her brother, and uncle. There were so many things to go over and everyone was so far apart. She wouldn't deny Gavin's parents the right to attend the ceremony and that's what she would have to do if she insisted it be held at Kara Keep. She had always wanted to wed at that grand castle with her father and mother at hand. Her parents or brother could not pack up and leave for a month; their businesses were too demanding. With raiders attacking from all directions no one was free to leave for an extended period of time. The wedding including travel there and back would require the better part of three weeks. Her final decision was to have the wedding here and send messengers to let the family know it had taken place. No one should or would have to travel as Gavin and she would visit within the year.

"When should we wed?" asked Morgana.

"Tomorrow," said Gavin.

"Oh no you are not pushing me into it that fast. Give me time to breathe."

"All right in a week then, you'll have lots of time to fix your hair."

"No."

"Why not? How long do you need?"

Morgana thought about it but saw no reason to delay. Her new life would start within the week.

"You are right. If we are going to do it why delay. Whenever your father can get things in place we will wed."

"I'll get started."

"Now?"

"Why not? You said if we're going to do it why delay?"

Morgana laughed and knew she was going to have fun with that man.

Two days later the duchess and the maids hustled her into the bathroom. They removed her clothes under protest; no one dressed or undressed a warrior. Short of slashing at them with her sword there was no way of stopping them so engrossed were they with the task at hand. They whisked her into a tub of steaming water; she almost passed out from the heat. They scrubbed her and washed her hair not once but three times. She resented all being done to her but would offend no one.

They pulled Morgana from the tub then dried her and lay her upon a table. They rubbed her body with oils and scents everywhere, making her scream a couple of times. They brushed and braided her hair then started to dress her. The shift came first, then the under gown, and on top of that, her wedding dress. Over it all they slipped on a mantel, then came the boots and gloves. Everything smelled fresh, clean, and was white in colour.

Morgana was led outside to a waiting carriage which looked as though it had just been painted white for the occasion. Two white horses with white harness were hitched to the front. She was taken to the village not far away and could see they had all prepared for a celebration. Cloths and coloured flags hung from the buildings. The village was alive with people everywhere too many to be from this hamlet alone; they must have come from farms and homesteads far away. As she approached the meeting hall more and more people appeared from allies and from behind and inside buildings along the street.

Morgana saw the reason for the high turnout; two wagons loaded with barrels of ale and tables filled with food nearby. Cups were freely filled and plates of cooking handed out. The carriage stopped and she was led into the hall, already filled.

Morgana was led down the aisle to the spot where Gavin stood waiting. Her left hand was bound to his right with a white cloth. A priest in white robes spoke to them in a language she couldn't understand. After a time he threw something that looked like grain.

"I declare thee wed."

The priest turned and left, Gavin kissed then swept Morgana into his arms. He carried her along the aisle as people cheered then set her in the carriage and sat beside her. The cheering was loud all the way along the street, both waving as they passed. Once free of the village Gavin galloped the horses back to the castle making her laugh at his haste. She giggled as they ran up the steps then shut the door behind them.

"Well we're married," said Gavin, a lump in his throat.

"Have you ever done it before?" asked Morgana.

"I've given everyone the impression I've had all the maids but no I haven't. What about you?"

"Oh no, I've saved myself for this special day, this special time."

"So what do you want to do next?"

"I think we should undress and jump into bed."

Morgana turned her back to Gavin then removed her wedding dress and under garments except for the shift. She turned to see Gavin nervously fumbling with the buttons on his pants. Morgana climbed into bed and pulled the cover high. Gavin jumped in next to her naked. After Gavin was undercover she slid the shift off and threw it on the floor.

They slept little but loved and talked a lot. Next morning Gavin took her to the brook where first they'd shared each others company. There upon the ground lay a large square of stone.

"What is that to be?" asked Morgana.

"That's to be our house, our own; it'll be small at first but..."

"Oh my God, when did you start it?"

"The day after we met. I got our stone mason to start putting it together."

"You are sure of yourself Gavin?"

"Just hoping that's all. That's all life is about, isn't it. Plans, work, and hope."

"And love."

"That above all."

Morgana loved his boyish charm and his simple approach to life and people. Her only doubts of him lay in those thoughts; would he grow with her or remain in that youthful world where he reigned unopposed.

Although with him the day long she could not get enough of him. They rode to the coast inspecting the warning fires they had arranged. Everything seemed in order, everyone on vigil watching the sea. At the castle they had almost fifty soldiers in all, their training going well. Wherever she went Morgana encouraged everyone to train and become familiar with the use of weapons. The bow and the spear she suggested would be the least costly and least time consuming. This would take time to nurture and results would not soon be forthcoming but in time local assistance would double their ability to deal with the threats from the sea.

The time passed, the stone mason setting walls to their house, summer in full swing. Morgana knew that the ice was gone in the northern straits and fiords. Raiders would soon sail south and possibly to their shores. She sent word to folk that this season of plenty included the coming thieves that would take all.

CHAPTER XX

It was the first time the castle woke to the new bell Morgana had installed. They were under attack from the sea. She pulled on her leathers and threw on her armour while watching Gavin do the same.

They raced to the stable and saddled their mounts. Bluko was already putting the men into line. Twenty-five would ride out and twenty-three would stay as castle guards. Bluko assumed first command so would continue to give the orders.

Morgana and Gavin were first through the gates. They raced toward the first signal fire blazing in the night. Before reaching it they could already see the next. Morgana had arranged them in proximity so if one was not started for one reason or another the next would be seen. After reaching the second the third was visible near the village.

Morgana strung her bow scanning the moonlit horizon for intruders. There was yet no reason to believe the villagers were in peril as the raiders could be further south. There was also no reason to believe that a threat actually existed at all. It was one of the weaknesses within the structure of a warning system; if a fisherman drunk on mead started his fire based on a false sighting all would be for nothing. But if that were the case nothing could ever be said. Fear of making a mistake could cost them more than the occasional error. They all needed to be drilled sporadically.

Next to the castle the village was the biggest target in the area. Morgana approached the hamlet with care then heard shouts and saw a building burst into flames. As she closed on the main street she saw mounted riders battling the villagers. It was not a false alarm, they'd come. She galloped toward the nearest building and tied Trinket to a pole.

As Morgana sunk to one knee she thrust three arrows into the ground before her. She picked her target and fired. Before her arrow found home she nocked another and released it toward a nearby raider. She repeated the action over and over again, Gavin beside her doing the same. When five raiders lay dead in the street they acknowledged the threat. With screams of rage and revenge they converged on their targets only to be stopped by Bluko and the twenty-five soldiers. Like a moving wall with lances held forward Bluko crushed the force of twelve that dared stand in his way. No raider surrendered as in their tradition fought to the last man.

"They brought horses," said Gavin.

"They do that but only when after larger targets. There were about fifteen so I believe it was a scouting party for a larger force yet to come," said Morgana.

"Do we look for them?" asked Gavin.

"We have no choice. We will scout ahead," said Morgana.

Morgana knew Captain Bluko would follow at a distance.

"What's the big target they're after, the village?" asked Gavin.

"No, the castle."

"They wouldn't have the nerve to siege that, would they?"

"Oh yes they would, they have taken bigger."

Morgana and Gavin rode south to the next fire that led them toward the coast. Another warning fire led them to a group of warriors bearing torches making no effort whatsoever to conceal themselves. There were over a hundred raiders on foot heading north as though they were masters here. They were obviously informed of Morland's weaknesses probably through previous raids and information extracted from slaves they'd taken. So why shouldn't they be confident? They outnumbered the castle guard by more than two to one. Morgana knew there was nothing to do but return to the castle and wait for a siege. She met Captain Bluko on the way back.

"Evacuate the village, tell them to go north of the castle," said Morgana.

"How many?"

"Over a hundred."

"What about hit and run attacks?"

"They carry full body shields for a siege so it will be hard to get them with bows and there are too many to move in close. They travel heavy with armour and weapons. They think there is nothing here to stop them."

Morgana and Gavin returned to the castle where she prepared all for a siege. Morgana had never in her young life been in a castle under attack but her father prepared her for it.

Captain Bluko returned and Morgana watched from the ramparts as the villagers marched north. Not long after the raiders showed themselves calmly setting up camp out of arrow range. The castle was to be their target and they'd had all winter long to plan their attack.

No one slept that night; they either paced the castle grounds or stood on the ramparts watching the enemy camp. Little was said all knowing what the coming day had in store for them.

The sun rose too early that day, most within the castle walls hoped it would never show itself at all. Within its amber glow the raiders prepared their first assault on the castle. Their strategy was simple; hidden behind full body shields they stormed the castle gate. They poured oil on the old timber and set it ablaze then ran back out of range. It was a costly attack on their part as archers killed close to ten, another five died when rocks were dropped on them from the ramparts. No one inside suffered.

The gates burned quickly and Morgana made no attempt to extinguish the flames; she'd expected it. The warriors cheered as the fire consumed the barriers and they fell. Two iron gates inside the opening were shut and chained together. It was a safety precaution Morgana saw fit to have made and installed; she started the gates' construction the second day after her arrival.

At a distance it looked as though the warrior's chiefs gathered. Four men stood in a circle waving their hands and shouting. It was something they hadn't counted on; Morgana was now sure their information was gathered the previous year as they knew nothing she'd changed. They knew about the signal fires when they landed but so what. So someone knew they were coming; they had a superior force. Morgana watched closely to see how they reacted.

Morgana couldn't believe her eyes; half the warriors left

and marched over the hill out of sight. The ones still camped feasted and drank as though celebrating a victory. What was going on she wondered? Was it a trap? Why would they do such a thing?

Morgana waited and watched for a time as by mid afternoon nothing had changed. Committing forty men to an attack would finish the ones there now. It may cost dearly, maybe even twenty of her own but she could do it if the others were truly gone.

"What do you think Bluko? Attack?"

"Where are the others, that's what we have to know to make a decision."

"Why would they cut their force in half? They're inviting attack," said Morgana.

"No, maybe not in their minds. These are brash men. Over confident and believe the men they've left behind can outfight the force inside the castle. They fear nothing."

"I am going out. If the others are not around we charge them. Ready forty men if you see fit."

Morgana saddled Trinket and saw Gavin saddling his mount.

"Gavin, you are not going. It is work for one. You cannot ride fast enough, you could get us both killed, stay here."

"I'm going and that's all there is to it."

"No you are not. Do you want me to have you bound?"

Gavin threw his bridle at the wall and rushed out of the stable. It had been their first argument; it was out of love for him that it took place.

Morgana rode toward the gates, the chains came off, and they opened before her. On the way out she looked down at Gavin's sad face hoping to put a smile on it later if there was a later for any of them. She had fought thoughts like those whenever they arose; had been taught by her father they came to everyone and to rise above them. Courage was not easily found and must be constantly sought after.

Morgana charged through the gates and veered left of the warriors then past them along the road to the village. She raced over a hill into the village beyond then slowed Trinket to a walk. She glared into abandoned buildings, no one in the street. At the end of the street stood the meeting hall where they had wed, the door bent and broken. She saw no one inside; they weren't here.

Morgana galloped west to the top of a hill; nothing here either. She rode east and found nothing then south for a time and then stopped. She stopped to think where they could be and concluded that they probably walked south to their ships for some unknown reason. Back to the castle she raced to an evening sun. She stayed wide of the attackers but slowed to get an accurate count; fifty-five men in all.

Morgana galloped through the gate and before her were forty men lances in hand ready to fight. Morgana gave Bluko a nod and with that the captain led the soldiers out of the gate. They followed in double file. His left arm extended and his men responded by forming to his left in a neat line as though standing for inspection. On his command they charged, a wall forty horses, wide lances, forward thundered toward the warrior's encampment.

The raiders stood as though frozen in surprise and did nothing but stare. One finally rallied the rest causing shields to rise and weapons drawn. The horses and spears met foot soldiers in a crash that sounded like a giant oak falling in the woods. Shields split, spears snapped as horses trampled men.

Morgana took advantage of the disorder caused by the attack and fired at targets not guarded by shields. The cavalry was on one side of the raiders and her on the other.

Half the raiders lay dead after the first volley as the soldiers lined for a second. Morgana lay back taking whatever targets offered themselves to her. Broadswords were drawn by the soldiers as the raiders gathered in a circle. On command the second round left most of the raiders dead and the third wiped out the rest to the last man.

The last light of the sun shone upon the surviving soldiers as they buried their dead, eight in all. Four were wounded; two would be minus a limb but would live. Malisa tended to the wounded and treated scrapes and cuts on the rest.

Morgana couldn't believe what had transpired. Some of the raiders were drunk and could barely stand. They'd come here expecting the castle to fall merely by their presence. Maybe the old castle would have but not the one she'd reinforced. They hadn't expected a trained army here where no knights graced the land.

The night was filled with sorrow for the dead, they would be missed. Gavin came to Morgana and wrapped his arms around her, no words were exchanged. She'd seen Gavin and Brent enter the battlefield but after that saw neither until it was over. She'd been too busy to look for either.

Not having slept the night before and exhausted from battle sleep came quickly for her that night. She woke in Gavin's arms, the first light of the sun creeping through the bedroom window. She woke Gavin and dressed then ran to the ramparts. The sun climbed high above the horizon and at noon the raiders returned. There were sixty men of which half carried a huge log. Five others carried barrels, probably mead.

They'd returned to the ship for mead, it was like a party for them. They came upon their dead comrades in total surprise. They dropped the log and raced through the camp turning the dead over in disbelief. The leader walked forward shaking his fist toward the castle.

Morgana had decisions to make so sought out Bluko.

"Do we go out there after them or stay in here? It is certain they will break down the gate and get in. Do we want to fight on horseback or on the ground?"

"I think both. We could put ten archers above and in front of the gate. Twenty-five men could be mounted and attack when they break in. They'll have to fight horse soldiers in front and archers behind."

"Good, that is what we will do."

They didn't have long to wait for the raider's attack, it was no secret they were on the way. Blood curdling screams filled the air as they raced toward the gate. Half carried the log and the other half the shields to cover themselves and the log bearers.

Morgana stood at the Iron Gate, an arrow nocked. She was looking for any error on their part, anything like a leg not shielded or a low shield. A man with a shield stumbled leaving the log bearer he covered in the open for a heartbeat, all the time she needed to put an arrow in his throat. Another arrow found a calf forcing the man to his knees. The log bearer behind tripping over him and likewise did the next and so on until the log fell to the ground.

That was a gift from the Gods, one she would never forget. She took advantage of the scrambling men and killed two; archers above killed four more. They struggled with shields and the log but finally started forward again, eight raiders lay dead.

Morgana backed away as the log smashed into the Iron Gate men above dropping rocks on the bearers, three more raiders fell to the ground. The gate held and that was another gift. They would have to back up and ram it again. Morgana knew the gate would not stand another attack so ran to her horse. Gavin moved near then drew his sword and smiled. Morgana smiled in return then pulled down the face shield on her helmet.

It sounded like a giant oak falling in the forest when the gate gave way. Chains flew and bent iron was flung across the yard. The remaining warriors rushed in yelling. Lancers charged, shields exploded, spears broke, and horses trampled over men. It was then that Morgana saw him, the big man Rolf, the slave trader she'd put an arrow into last winter. She dismounted and took aim but a soldier and his horse blocked the way. Rolf pulled the man from his horse and rammed his broadsword into the soldier's stomach under the chest plate. Rolf mounted the soldier's horse and called for all to retreat. Morgana aimed and fired but her arrow bounced off his armour.

Morgana ran toward Rolf then stopped as her stomach melted. She was unable to move, to look away from the soldier Rolf had killed. It was Gavin. Morgana told herself she was a warrior and tried to hold back tears but failed. She ripped off her helmet and crashed to her knees beside Gavin rubbing his cheek begging him to wake. She looked at his wound then quickly away; men did not survive wounds such as those.

When Morgana realised Gavin would never wake, when she knew he was forever gone, she went after his killer. Anger and hate boiled inside while she scanned the castle grounds. Gavin's killer was nowhere to be found. The last of the raiders fled through the gate as she mounted Trinket to follow. Outside she watched a man disappear over a hill. It was Rolf on Gavin's horse. Twenty-five or so warriors followed on foot to the ships waiting along the coast. She looked back at what remained of the castle guard, only twenty-five battle weary soldiers. The raiders were beaten and would leave them; she would loose no more comrades giving pursuit of a defeated foe.

Brent rode to her side, tears in his eyes and lips quivering.

"Stay at the castle Bluko. We are going after Rolf."

They rode fast avoiding the warriors on foot. Through the village and along the road they raced but no sign of Rolf. He had a head start on a good mount. He would not pace Gavin's horse and ride at a dead run until he arrived at his ships or his mount foundered. Morgana couldn't do that to Trinket, couldn't risk killing her in hope of revenge. It wouldn't bring Gavin back, nothing would. She made herself a promise on that ride, one she would repeat to herself over and over again, she was going to kill Rolf if not today then soon. If she'd done her job right the first time and killed Rolf Gavin would still be alive.

It was half a day's ride to the sea at a normal pace but they would reach it in half that time at a run. Not far ahead she could see Gavin's horse on shore and a ship rowing out to sea. Twenty oars dug into the water as they moved away from shore then a sail raised, the vessel fading from sight.

Morgana and Brent rode into the fishing village not far away and retrieved torches and oil. There were three ships left on shore, they set two ablaze. Her father had told her to never leave raiders stranded as trapped they would be forced to spread out and kill for survival. Twenty-five maniacs running loose on the countryside would cause havoc for a year. She burned the other two as she wanted the price for their attack to be high. They'd made nothing this trip and would not be hasty to repeat their mistake.

They returned to the castle that evening the stench of death still in the air. Most of the bodies had been taken away including Gavin's. Morgana followed Brent to the cellar where the bodies were prepared. Other bodies lay in wait as loved ones sobbed over them in sorrow. Morgana told herself that she was going to set an example to the rest, she would show them how to let go with dignity. She was strong, a warrior, and a leader. She willed herself not to shed any tears but her loved one was gone. She screamed loud as she could, the pain was impossible to bear.

The funerals of all who fell took place at noon of the next day. Morgana's tears ceased after the earth covered Gavin's remains. She hoped he was in a better place then a minute later cursed him for leaving her alone.

The next few days were the hardest of her life, sometimes almost forgetting, sometimes starting to laugh, and then tears would flow again. She went to the brook and looked at her house almost built. She avoided her room, the place where they'd first made love. Morland was an ugly place when she'd first arrived; it turned into a world full of beauty after Gavin came into her life. It now turned ugly again.

Morgana made a decision; she would return to Kara Keep, there was nothing for her here but sorrow. Everywhere she looked stood Gavin's ghost.

Captain Bluko found love of his own while he was here so would stay. Only three soldiers from her original escort stilled lived and they also asked to stay with the captain. Malisa volunteered to remain as the wounded were still in need of her. Morgana would return alone. She loaded a pack horse and saddled Trinket, said her good byes and left.

CHAPTER XXI

Morgana rode from the castle and did not look back. Her only reason for staying in this dreary land was gone. She slowed Trinket to a walk and Brent was beside her.

"I am leaving alone Brent. Good bye."

"What if you break a leg or something? You'll die."

"Maybe I want to."

"Well, I'll ride along and if something happens and you want to be left alone to die then I'll let you. But you'll have a choice if I'm here."

"I cannot stop you from following but it will do you no good, I will never want you, you will never replace Gavin."

Brent did not answer, did not say a word, and only hung his head low. She hated it when he sulked but right now would probably hate anything he did. She'd been hard on him but wanted no advances, especially from him. She didn't really like the man and liked less the idea of riding and camping with him. Morgana had wanted to ride on her own and sort out her life along the way.

Brent was right about one thing: any mishap along the way could end her life if alone. Maybe he would stay out of the way and keep quiet; he was inclined to be that way in any case.

It wasn't long and they were on the road east to Dorville. Four days or so and she would see Edward and Andrew. That night setting up camp Brent got in her way. When she looked for the flint and stone to start the fire, it was gone. Fearing she had forgotten to pack it searched high and low. He had it. She searched for meat and bread, he already had it out.

"Look, you do it all or I do it all, you are getting in the way."

"Sorry, all right, you do it all, and then you'll have no more complaints."

Morgana left Morland due to constant reminders of Gavin and now his brother was here. Maybe she shouldn't forget, maybe she should remember and let time soften the blows.

"Was he always that way? You know, good with people," asked Morgana making her voice warm and friendly.

"Since two. He was born with charm."

"Were you close?"

"Oh yes, despite our differences, he needed me for some things and I needed him for others."

"What was his main job on the farm before I came along?"

"He was the one who settled problems; he would get people talking to each other to settle arguments. He was a judge of sorts, I guess."

"Yes, he would be good at that."

"He was a hard worker but seldom did the same thing two days in a row."

"What was your job at the farm?"

"Lately, to arrange a trade partnership with your brother. I'm good with numbers and barter so did that."

"Are you here on business or to protect me?"

"I don't need to see Edward until after harvest time. Do you think I'd let you ride off alone."

"So you will turn back after we arrive at Dorville?"

"No I'll ride with you to Kara Keep."

"Why?"

"You visited us so I'm going to visit you."

That hit Morgana in the face like a shovel. She didn't know how to react and would have to think about it. Return with her dead husband's brother? She felt like screaming at him, he was so calm about it. Would it do any good? One thing for sure she would have to get an escort, couldn't show up at Kara Keep with him alone. What would that look like? Camping under the stars with an ex-suitor?

The trip to Dorville was eventless and thoughts about the past months refused to leave her alone. She was oblivious to nature and its sounds and all else around her. In her present state she would be easy prey for highwaymen or raiders as the ability to concentrate failed her. She would think of Gavin and her mind would go blank refusing to do anything with thoughts of him.

Morgana would always see his body as she'd seen it after the battle, legs twisted, wide dead eyes, and blood. Even when having thoughts about her wedding night, eventually she would see his dead body and then Rolf. The last person she wanted in her mind was Rolf but sooner or later thinking of Gavin she would see his killer as well.

Morgana was alerted by the metallic sound of a sword being drawn from its sheath and twisted both ways looking for danger. Brent had drawn his broadsword and stared down the road toward the east. Two traders leading pack mules rounded one of the many bends. One nodded with a toothless smile and the other raised his hand in greeting. Brent nodded and returned the sword to its sheath. Morgana was glad someone was alert and returned to thoughts of dread. Round and Round she went refusing to leave that world behind yet having no control over the pictures coming into her mind.

"Can you please help me Brent?" she sobbed.

Brent jumped from his horse and stopped hers then pulled Morgana crying from the saddle. He held her tight, his tears running into her hair. She stood for an eternity thankful for the touch of another then wrapped her arms around him not wanting to move.

Morgana's sobs waned as Brent set up camp early that night doing all the work and shaking his finger at her whenever she rose to help. After eating and cleanup they talked and held each other the night long. If she had ever been vulnerable to the advances of a man tonight was such a night. She needed to be with someone and would pay whatever price was necessary for his company without regard to afterthought. He only held her, never an inappropriate touch. They shared the same sorrow and helped each other through the long night and then the next.

Dorville Castle loomed before her and she rode through the open gates her best friend, Brent, close behind. Edward greeted both.

"Edward, listen to me, my Gavin's been killed in an attack by raiders," she sobbed.

Edward said nothing, only pulling her close. She cried as he hugged her and like a week of storms her sorrow ceased. Feeling silly she lightly laughed as though returning from another world. A weight had been lifted from her by some unknown force. Her big brother and best friend were both there, nothing could hurt her now.

Their stay only lasted two days; Morgana needing to see

her father again. He was the knight in her life, her guardian, and mentor.

"I will get an escort ready for you," said Edward.

"We will be fine dear brother," said Morgana giving Brent a smile.

Morgana rode with Brent at her side chatting about nothing and everything. He certainly was intelligent; he seemed to know something about everything. Time passed quickly both talking of family and friends and odd nature of some. They soon left the flat farm lands behind as hills grew taller and rocks larger in size.

That night at the campfire Morgana knew she would have to set things clear in Brent's mind.

"I want you to know that you are a dear friend but that is the extent of it. I do not have the same feelings for you as I had for Gavin and will probably never have. We can be only that, just friends."

"I know so be it. I'll take whatever you give to me dear lady and offer whatever you need or desire."

"You must find another, is what I am trying to tell you. Do not waste your life chasing me. I may never love another again. I fear another loss like Gavin would make me insane."

"You'll never wed again?"

"Only if I find another soul to love would I even consider such a thought."

"Are you going to live at the keep again?"

"For now."

"You know I've loved you from the first. I'm reluctant to step out of your life."

"I will not force you out only suggest you find someone else."

"Then I'll stay for now. Let's see what takes place."

Woolly beasts grazed on both sides of the road, dogs barking as Morgana and Brent came their way. They were in sheep country where her mother reigned serving the people as they served her. The duchess Amanda was loved by all as she worked bringing commerce to the north.

On top of the next hill Kara Keep came into full view. Morgana was home.

"Wow, that's unbelievable, who would ever attempt to take that?" said Brent.

"No one yet. Come we will be there for dinner my friend."

Morgana watched as Brent marvelled at the sight.

"Those cliffs are high enough to kill a man if he fell. The walls aren't really needed, mountains and cliffs all around," said Brent.

They wound their way up the path to the front gate which opened as they neared.

"It's lady Morgana."

She heard shouts from the ramparts and throughout the castle as it echoed from the walls.

Stable boys rushed to gather their horses welcoming Morgana and Brent. She was met by her father who'd come out to see what all the shouting was about. Her knight lifted her from the ground and spun her in crazy circles.

"This must be Gavin," said Damon.

"No father, Gavin was killed in a raid; we will speak of it later. This is his brother Brent, my dearest friend," said Morgana for the first time without shedding a tear.

Morgana's father was silent and she could see he was uncomfortably searching for words. She followed her father inside and freshened up for dinner. They'd not given her bedroom to anyone else so still had the things she had left behind. Dinner was an unavoidable discomfort as all knew of her new husband's fate. They said little afraid to speak in fear of uttering the wrong words.

"Please listen to me everyone. My husband Gavin was killed almost a month ago. I have shed my tears and oh God I miss him so but life must go on. Please say whatever comes to mind. I cannot mourn him forever and will not even try. I am all right."

With that came a flurry of questions about Brent's lands to the west and the raider's threat.

Morgana lay in bed and heard a knock on the door.

"Come in father."

Since a child her father would visit her to wrap up the day as much for himself as her. They shared the same thoughts, likes and dislikes.

"How are things here these days?" asked Morgana.

"Oh, not too bad actually. There is group of raiders trying to settle in the north east. I set out in two days to drive them away."

"I am going with you."

"It is too soon. Sleep and relax for a time. I will see you tomorrow."

"Father, please come back. Please talk to me the way we used to. I need you so."

"What is wrong?"

"I need to kill a raider, Roth; he is the one who killed Gavin."

"All right, you will go with us. I do not know what I was thinking; you are going to go wherever you want anyway.

I could not stop you two years ago and certainly will not now."

"Thank you father. I think Brent will also want to go."

"Does he know how to fight?"

"Like a knight father, like a knight."

They talked a while and he tucked her in like he used to when she was but a child. He left with a smile.

CHAPTER XXII

Morgana rode to the head of the column to join her father and Brent. One hundred frontier guards joined the knight. They were on route to destroy a settlement built by raiders who were no longer content to plunder but also sought to conquer. They wanted to extend their lands into the property of others free of taxes and laws. Her father had destroyed several of these compounds springing up across the country. Morgana would seek out Rolf if he was there and hoped that either she or Brent could kill him.

It was a two day ride to reach the sod and wood fortress. According to a trapper only fifty warriors guarded the compound. From their home base the Norlanders would trade if possible but failing that would steal.

Sir Roth rode toward the compound, all one hundred soldiers at his rear. He made no attempt to hide his purpose. He was here to drive them back from where they came. He called two knights forward and ordered soldiers to gather dead branches. The branches were tied in a huge bundle and ropes to pull them handed the knights. They dragged the bundles toward the front gate, arrows bouncing harmlessly off their full armour. Their horses were covered with thick wool blankets which arrows also failed to penetrate. Once at the front gate the knights pushed the brush toward the barriers then set them ablaze. Sir Roth's archers prevented the raiders from extinguishing the flames.

The gates burned and fell to ground. Archers stood around campfires lighting the oil cloths tied to the ends of their arrows and fired them burning into the buildings beyond. The huts made of sod and wood smoked and were slow to burn.

Later that day when the smoke cleared only sod mounds remained. Sir Roth ordered an attack but before anyone charged a line of raiders walked through the burned out front gate and surrendered.

Morgana and Brent searched for Rolf but he was not among them. They questioned the leader who denied ever knowing the man. They led the raiders toward the sea to the place where their ships were beached. They watched them row from shore then sail away. They were out of the way and no lives lost, all fighting had been avoided. The north men's punishment for trespassing was the loss of their goods and possessions to fire. They would not soon return.

That was her father's way but Morgana knew things would have been different had Rolf been there. And what would happen to the others on either side if she'd killed him? A blood bath could have been the result. She and Brent would have to find a way to separate him from others.

They all rode back to the keep and arrived two days later weary and unclean. Amanda, Morgana's mother waited wearing a grim look on her face.

"You know I do not like you going on missions with your father. A hunting trip yes, but not fighting raiders. It is no place for a woman," said Amanda.

"It is time you were aware of the fact I am not like you or

Edward, I am no wall flower. I have killed more raiders than most of your soldiers," said Morgana.

"I am not a wall flower either young lady. There are other ways a woman can serve king and country without standing sword in hand beside men. The business of tending castles and lands is as rewarding as winning a battle. Women are more suited to the first than the latter."

"Oh mother, I know what you have done here. You are a legend among our people but dear mother your way is not in my heart. My way lays in father's footsteps, not yours."

Amanda hugged her daughter, "Take care dear. There is only sorrow for a mother who outlives her daughter. And maybe that is what I am thinking about, myself. Maybe I am being selfish."

Morgana searched for her father and found him in the stable.

"I have to find Rolf and separate him from other raiders then kill him. How do I go about doing that?" asked Morgana.

"First of all your obsession will only result in your death. Second, he could be anywhere right now. Maybe in some northern fiord out of your reach. I know he has a winter camp in the islands to the north but which one or where, I don't know."

"So I must wait until winter?" said Morgana, more of a statement than a question.

"Unless someone else kills him first, that's where he'll be."

"Who would know where his camp lies?"

"Maybe Rogun, I know they traded before your mother made peace with him."

"Well that's it then I find Rogun and find out where he stays."

Morgana and Brent sought out Melanie the village healer a friend to Rogun and were given the location of his camp. They slept the night in beds and rode north in the glare of the rising sun.

The north was a land of steep hills and rocks more rugged than the sheep grazing valleys at Kara Keep. Few roads existed and those that did narrowed to trails. It was mid summer yet the nights in the hills were cool further chilled by winds from the nearby sea.

At the campfire that night Morgana and Brent spoke of many things but seldom about Gavin of late. Morgana didn't avoid the subject but had few things to say to another of that short past. She would love no other as much as Gavin that she knew. That magic and fire of youth, that first time alone with a man would never come again. That experience would forever bind her to Gavin. She would never be a maiden again and never that innocent or that naïve. That experience only happened once in everyone's life, Gavin was hers.

Next morning Rogun's camp lay before them, people running in greeting to Morgana. The sheep given them by her mother grazed around the camp, guarded by herding dogs, another gift.

"Hello Rogun, I need your help," said Morgana.

"You have whatever I can give."

"Do you know where Rolf camps in winter?"

"It's not hard to find. The first island north, in the southeast is his camp. You'll always see smoke from there."

"How many men with him?"

"Oh that's hard to say as it differs, fifty at most."

"How do I get across?"

"You don't seek to trade do you?"

"Nothing that friendly."

"Then find Tamus along the southeast shore of this land. He's a mercenary with no love for Rolf and has ships to take you there. He's not cheap and will ask for a lot of gold in return for what he does. He's the only one I know that would help you with that."

"Thank you, we will start south again in a couple of days. For now I want to visit and show Brent this northern land."

"Your company and words of the south are always welcome here."

Morgana stayed two days then returned to Kara Keep. Amanda approached her with news from the south two messengers had delivered the day before.

"The king seeks your audience as well as that of Brent."

CHAPTER XXIII

Sir Roth would take Morgana and Brent south-east to see the king. It was mid summer so the trip was dry and hot with only an occasional shower.

"What would the king want of us father?"

"I don't know it could be anything but probably something to do with the raiders in Morland. He's plagued by them himself on his east shore."

"Maybe he needs our help to drive them out," said Brent with a chuckle.

"Hah, he has two hundred knights and five thousand soldiers. You two as good as you are would turn no tide in battle," said Sir Roth.

"I think it is our advice that he needs," said Morgana.

"In two days we'll find out," said Sir Roth.

They arrived at the King's castle, the grandest palace Morgana had ever seen, white walls surrounding ivory towers. A courtyard brushed clean as they entered, not a scrap of anything blowing in the breeze. A fountain sprayed water into pools below where swans gracefully paddled to and fro. Pigeons cooed on ledges while finches flittered through the bushes. The works of man and nature melded to create a scene suitable for a king.

Soldiers escorted them to the highest structure in the

square. Their horses were taken and rooms assigned to them. Sir Roth was not on the roster but would be seen at the same time as Morgana. They changed and dined then rushed to the Great Hall by nervous aids of the king. Their time had come and the king could not be kept waiting it seemed.

"Brent McBoden." cried an aid to the king.

Morgana looked toward the weary king signing a document and giving it to an aid.

"Brent McBoden will from this day forward be known as Sir Brent McBoden for his bravery in dealing with the raiders in Morland," shouted the aid.

"Morgana Roth I recognize your efforts to train soldiers and I acknowledge your aid in driving an enemy from our lands. No position exists for a woman's achievements in matters of war. Our highest award will be given you and you are from this day considered a "Lady of the Realm", Lady Morgana," said the king.

Everyone in attendance clapped, her father and Brent beaming.

"My condolences to you for the loss of your husband. I also look forward to your union with Duke Ascott," said the king.

Morgana stepped forward to speak but her father's hand clutched her arm tightly so she said nothing.

"Damon Roth, your majesty," yelled an aid.

The king merely crossed his arms and waited for Sir Roth to speak.

"With respect your majesty, at your request Morgana my daughter went to Morland to choose one of two suitors named by you, and so she did. She is widowed but has already pledged her hand in marriage to the other of your choosing Sir Brent McBoden," said Sir Roth.

Again Morgana stepped forward to speak and again her father gripped her forearm so tightly it ached.

The king was a man with heavy thoughts on his mind and a look of anger on his brow. He finally raised his head and stared at Sir Roth as though staring at a traitor.

"So be it then as I first decreed. I commend you on your choice Lady Roth," said the king and rose to his feet.

"You are all dismissed," shouted an aid.

Although it was steadily raising Morgana held her anger at bay then outside in the midst of the square she exploded.

"What was that all about? What are you doing to me? Whose Duke Ascott and I did not, I repeat did not give my hand to Brent father dear."

"I came here not only of free will but also at the request of your mother. We both feared what the king would do with you after Gavin's death. You have become a legend in this country and a prize coveted by all noblemen. The king needs a stronger alliance with Ascott. You were to be the trade. The Duke is older than I, fat and bald."

"So I would have said no. I have that right as Lady of the Realm."

"He would pressure with increased levies on our lands. All including shepherds would suffer and you would sooner or later relinquish."

"Why Brent? He's Gavin's brother. I am sorry Brent you are a friend but no more than that, not a mate."

"For that reason your mother and I selected Brent, because you're friends. You can work out some form of relationship. I trust him and so do you. Who else would you have me choose other than you best friend?"

"Why did you not tell me of your fears?"

"Because you would have fought them and may not even have come south to the king. You would have spoiled the outcome as it now stands. You're a fighter but some things you cannot fight and must give into if not the way of the king then a compromise."

"I am sorry father and know you to be at truth in this matter. So dear Brent I see we are to be wed after all."

"You'll live a life of your own choosing. I take nothing you will not freely give and offer all I can," said Brent.

"We will talk of it later. For now let us walk and see the sights, and thank you knights, the both of you for coming to my rescue and saving me from the clutches of a fat old Duke."

They enjoyed the sights and sampled cuisine from vendor's shops. Sir Roth left Morgana and Brent in a park so he could visit old friends.

"I cannot love you as I did Gavin. I do not know if I can ever bed you as a wife should. I do not know if I will ever bear your children."

"I am doing this to save you from being wed to a stranger. We'll see what the future brings. For now let's just concentrate on being friends."

"I am sorry but a part of me is empty and I do not know whether I will ever be whole again."

The next day Sir Damon Roth, Sir Brent McBoden, and Lady Morgana McBoden rode north-east to find a mercenary named Tamus. They stopped at several villages along the coast and found the mercenary. A deal was struck and sure enough as Rogun had said the man demanded a king's ransom for his part. They would meet at a village in the far north-east close to Rolf's camp early this winter.

All three returned to Kara Keep their meeting with the mercenary only two months away.

CHAPTER XXIV

The countryside was a thousand shades of red and gold; a cold north wind blew leaves from the trees leaving bare branches reaching for the sky. Clouds hid the sun from view and days grew shorter all the while. Squirrels and chipmunks raced to store the last fruits of the year. Fat bears and raccoons readied their dens for the long winter's sleep. The dark season was on its way.

Morgana checked her bow eyeing the string for wear. She dumped her quiver of arrows on the table and one by one made sure they would all fly true. She sharpened her sword and dagger and last the two knives hidden inside her boots. She left two arrows on the table and returned the rest to the quiver. She wanted no misses this time, hunting Rolf. That's the way she viewed her task; hunting the slave trader who'd killed her man.

Morgana arrived at the stables and smiled at Brent their horses already saddled. They would take a packhorse to the village along the coast two days away. They left through the north gate and another horse fell in behind. Sitting upon it was Sir Roth.

"It is only Brent and I that need to go, father."

"Gavin was one of the family when you two wed. Anyone who as much as lays a hand on family will answer to me."

"Yes father," said Morgana with a sly smile.

They said little on the two day journey to the sea. They knew a battle was coming their way whether Rolf was in the camp or not. The mercenaries they'd hired would take them to the island and stand behind them on their attack.

The village came into view and soon they entered. They stabled their horses and met the men for hire already there. Hands were shaken and the deal sealed when Brent gave them the remaining payment in gold.

Morgana stepped into the Dragonship as it lay beached upon the shore. She looked about, her first time in any vessel, it was about twenty paces long and ten wide. It was made of dark grey wood, a large mast dead centre held a sail rolled up and wide as the ship was long. On command the sailors pushed the vessel into the sea and climbed aboard. With oars set into the side they rowed from shore. Once clear the sail was hoisted and they were underway.

The ship heaved into the air, the waves reaching high. Not much could be seen as cloud and snow obstructed the view. Morgana clutched tight knowing she would soon be sick and was. She'd never felt damp cold like this, the strong wind reaching deep inside. She fought to breathe as anxiety held her in its icy grip. The vast sea was all around and she was in this tiny vessel thrashing out of control. She wondered what was keeping them afloat. Their destination seemed almost out of reach, the distant shore looked as though it crept away. Then as all things good or bad their journey came to end. The ship slammed into shore and dug its way into the sandy beach.

They'd landed west of the raider's camp and moved quickly along the shore. There was little daylight left and they must find Rolf tonight or would have to spend the night ashore. Smoke bellowed from the huts and men moved about the compound busy at their daily chores. Morgana and Brent took the lead, her father not far behind. They both counted and whispered numbers to each other, thirty they agreed but how many in the huts? It looked as though their evening meal was in progress and all would be present for that. Morgana's eyes searched yet could not find Rolf. He was not among them so should they abandon their attack? Then taking command Tamus the mercenary leader started his assault. Raiders without armour fell quickly to the arrows and swords of his men.

Out of a hut far away from shore ran a man with a woman in his hand. Morgana tapped Brent on the shoulder and they gave chase. A defending raider stood in Morgana's path and Brent jumped in between, a fight to the death underway. Morgana raced after the man following him into the woods. He clutched the woman's arm half dragging her at times. Morgana had an arrow nocked but was unable to release it in the woods, too many trees in the way.

The man was crossing a stream when the woman fell. He pulled the woman to her feet and as he did Morgana saw his face, it was Rolf. She pulled back the bowstring and aimed. He stood his ground the woman before him as a shield, his sword at her throat. Morgana walked close trying to put an arrow in his face. She was only a few paces away when he shoved the slave at her. Morgana released the bowstring as she was knocked to the ground. Rolf swung his sword cutting across the slave's back.

Morgana pulled herself from under the woman's bleeding body and tried to scramble to her feet but slipped and landed on her back. Rolf stood over her and Morgana knew she would be his next victim. His sword pulled high to strike when she saw the blade of another weapon pierce through his chest. His face turned to horror as he fell to the ground. Rolf was dead thank the God's thought Morgana. She looked beyond him and saw Brent ten paces away. "How did you do that?" asked Morgana.

"I just learned how to throw it," said Brent.

Morgana saw blood dripping from his right hand. He'd grasped the sharp blade and thrown it like a spear.

"You fool," said Morgana.

"You're still alive."

Morgana tore strips from the dead slave's dress and bandaged his hand. He retrieved his sword and she her bow.

When they returned to the compound all the raiders were dead as Rolf. The mercenaries ate food their victims had no time to finish and walked about collecting valuables.

"Rolf is dead father."

"And you. Is revenge enough?" asked Sir Roth.

"I could not go on with my life while he lived. Gavin would be alive today had I killed him last winter. It needed to be done that is all."

"Don't blame yourself. It may have been Gavin's time to die," said Brent.

That night Morgana nursed Brent's hand and she sat close. She thought about Gavin and knew that loving man would not want her to live on her own in honour of his memory. She thought he would want her to wed and raise little warriors with another kind soul, who would better fit that role than his brother. Brent had sacrificed all for her, did not leave her side for even a day. He'd killed Rolf and saved her life all on one wild gamble throwing his sword in that way. He was as rare a gift in his way as Gavin. She would gladly wed him and bear his children.

With Rolf dead Morgana could let go of the past, let go of Gavin. That part of her life had ended with the raider's death. She had softened to Brent from the start, when he refused to let her ride to the keep alone. She'd tried to hurt him but nothing would make him go. Then after the king tried to wed her to Ascot he was willing to marry her and tie up the rest of his life with nothing in return. No heirs, no future but he was still willing to be with her. She wanted to move on and who would she move on with, Brent. Who else would it be? He would never let her down.

The morning brought another wild ride in the ship Morgana's way. Up and down then over the side her breakfast went, the one she shouldn't have eaten. Even bitter events come to an end although this one took a long time. The ship beached itself on the village shore almost throwing her overboard. She climbed from the vessel vowing never again to sail, her love was for horses and land not the unfriendly sea.

They shook hands with Tamus and said their good byes. They retrieved their horses and set out for Kara Keep. The return journey was full of silly talk mostly from her. She was in a giddy mood, her new future about to begin. She laughed and smiled looking at Brent often, his face puzzled. Morgana had made up her mind that future happiness lay with that man. Had she shared her thoughts with him he would be happy as well. That would happen soon.

When they returned to the keep Malisa was back, brought home by four guards. The wounded were healed and she was needed no more.

Amanda prepared a wedding like her own at the village

inn for Morgana and Brent. The white carriage and flowers the same as she'd had. Her father gave Morgana's hand to Brent as all cheered and looked on. Women cried and men clapped as they left the inn and took the carriage back to the keep.

After the wedding the first night was finally theirs. Brent was all thumbs as Gavin had been. She had the advantage and would not tease but help. She guided his hands, he was gentle and kind, all a woman could ask. In life decisions had to be made and seldom did one get exactly what they wanted, life was compromise.

Time moved on the weeks then the months. She was pregnant and tried to be cheerful but the pain the last months was hard to bear. Clorisa showed a sad face at times, she knew that the old woman was aware of something yet would not say. Amanda her mother looked brave, too brave she thought.

Two weeks before the baby was due Morgana went into labour. Morgana died like a warrior that night saving the life of a little girl, her own. She pushed and held on until the child breathed and cried. She held her and with her last breath whispered "Rhianna" to Brent. She closed her eyes and was no more.

PART THREE

RHIANNA

CHAPTER XXV

Rhianna McBoden dabbed the sweat off her neck as she rode beside her father to Kara Keep. The summer day was more humid than hot and quite uncomfortable wearing her thick travelling apparel. Looking up at the darkening clouds she knew they would soon be drenched so put the handkerchief back in her pocket.

They were returning from Morland one of the two places she called home. At eighteen years old she had travelled throughout the country with her father Sir Brent McBoden. It was a dream come true for a young woman riding beside a knight from place to place, one adventure after another.

Rhianna was listening to her father's loving words as he talked of her mother Morgana.

"Your mother trained not only me but every soldier in Morland as well you know. Did I ever tell you that?" said Brent.

He had several times over the years and she always answered, "No that's one I've never heard so tell me."

And beaming with joy he would tell her another tale of the mother she never knew. Rhianna never tired of his stories and he never tired of telling.

"She was the best archers in the land and few bested her with a broadsword, and beautiful, oh, she was lovely. Where do you think you got your looks from, not me that's for sure," said Brent.

Her father would add that little ending to every tale making her smile. There was nothing but love in his words and sorrow crossed his brow when he stopped, as he did now. She would not push him at times like these, just let him be to deal with a loss long past.

They sat on the roots of an elm tree in a grove not far from the road neither saying a word only watching the rain. A summer shower was in progress all around, the trees sheltering them from the worst. It was the kind of rain that consumes the air making it hard to breathe; a downpour that came and went in no time at all and soon they were on their way.

Rhianna tried to live up to the image they painted of her mother but failed with regret. She could use a bow and with it put an arrow into a tree but not to a single point within. Rhianna could swing a sword but not with enough force to hurt much less kill. Her father always said that with a sword she was only dangerous to herself. She was not to be the legendary warrior equal to her mother, so be it.

Neither was Rhianna the business woman the like of her grandmother. Rhianna did not live under the shadow of those two opposites nor could she live off their fame. She was a woman of her own and would find her place in life as they had.

On their return from Morland they had stopped at Dorville castle to see her uncle Edward. He had taken over the family business interests in the south after his uncle Andrew passed away two years before leaving no heirs. Edward himself had never married and gave no excuse for his reluctance to do so. No family member had ever pushed for explanation even in a friendly way. He was not the kind of man who shared his personal life or thoughts with anyone. He was truly like his mother Amanda whom Rhianna used to call "the iron lady" when she was small. Her whole life she had seen neither shed a tear.

The stay over at Dorville was as usual filled with feasts and talk of business matters beyond Rhianna's scope. She would leave the men to chat and visit with Mary her great uncle Andrew's wife. He'd married her knowing she was barren and would give no heirs so sparked Rhianna's interest as love would be his only reason for doing so. She listened to Mary's tales of the family; stories of Grandmother Amanda and her mother Morgana.

Rhianna and Brent left the castle three days later and resumed the journey home. Her father seemed to distance himself from the lives of his kin in Morland. His parents still looked after the family business interests which he seemed to want no part of. He'd roamed the country tying together all the farming interests in the south, west, and north. He was an organizer for trade and culture. He tied people and land together as one. Rhianna was his apprentice and learned his art with ease having talents inherited by him. That's where Rhianna believed her future lay in the binding of land and people.

They camped that night beside a small lake, the fish snatching bugs in mid air. The sun slid behind the hills as they gathered wood for a fire. Rhianna always cooked as she knew her father hated doing so.

"You're like your mother when we camp. She used to hate it if I touched anything and let me know it."

"Would you ever go back to Morland and look after the

farms there, you know, when you get older I mean?" asked Rhianna.

"No I'm not a farmer. I'm a traveller, don't like to stay in one place for long," said Brent.

"Why do you spend so much time at Kara Keep then? I never asked and maybe should not."

"That's all right. I feel closer to Morgana there. I like Amanda and Damon, and, well they're like a link to Morgana's spirit. I don't know how to explain it better than that. I feel her at Kara Keep, nowhere else, only there, I guess because she died there."

"You must have truly loved her."

"From the first day and like nothing else on earth. I miss her so much, did I ever tell you about the time her and Gavin followed the raiders to the coast?"

"No you did not, so tell."

And he would start again to bring Morgana back to life for another night then suddenly stop. She wondered if he suffered during those quite times or just had private thoughts.

"Father, there is something that I have thought a lot about lately and I just have to ask you so please be honest when you answer, please I have to know."

"What is it sweetheart?"

"Do you ever blame me for mother's death? I mean she gave her life for me. And sometimes when you talk about her you just shut me out after."

She watched his eyes go wide as he straightened and stared at her, tears streaked down his cheeks. Rhianna was sorry she had asked.

"Never have I or would I ever blame you for her death. I was there when you were born. With her last breath she gave you a name. I was the first to hold you and have loved you since that day. Morgana was the kind of woman that would have died for any one of the children in the village not only kin.

"There's payment for the good memories I have of the short time I spent with her. That payment is sooner or later I always see her die."

He hid his head in his hands and she hugged him tight.

"I am sorry it is something I should never have asked."

"No, if you thought what you did it had to be cleared up; you couldn't live forever with that. I should have kept some of those black thoughts to myself and not shown them around you."

Rhianna sobbed with him and regretted bringing up that subject; it was something she should have kept to herself. She fell asleep later that night and was awakened by her father as he was saddling the horses and breaking camp. It was his chore in return for the cooking she did the night before.

Later that day Kara Keep appeared on the horizon and Rhianna felt that strange attraction to the castle and the lands beyond. It felt as though the spirit of Morgana protected these lands as much in death as she had in life.

On entering the castle Rhianna saw an entourage of gentlemen talking to her grandmother in the great hall.

"Well we are honoured but as I said before it is Rhianna's decision, not mine. It is she who will decide to attend," said Amanda.

"Attend what?" said Rhianna.

"The King wants you to attend him at court. We are to escort you young lady," said the emissary.

"Am I to be taken as a prisoner? You say he wants and that

you are here to escort. Do I have a choice?" asked Rhianna as her temper flared.

"Of course you do. I merely wanted to point out the king's desire and our availability to see you safely there."

"Then my answer is no. I have only just returned from Morland and wish to see family and friends," said Rhianna.

"May I further entice you then by telling you the king is in the process of choosing a wife and you are one of the women he wishes to meet. Your beauty is renowned throughout the land and he wishes to meet the owner of the legend."

Rhianna's anger turned to rage at the thought. The old king had passed away two years before and the new successor was rumoured to be a womanizer.

"I won't be paraded before him like some kind of prize cow. If he truly seeks my hand he may attend it here," she said trying to contain herself but failing at the end as her voice turned into a slur.

"No, now, do you know what you're asking? We cannot return and tell him that," said the emissary.

"Then tell him whatever you want or take me to him in chains," slurred Rhianna.

"Lady Amanda what is your word on this?" asked the emissary.

"I've already given you my word. We stand behind Rhianna."

"So do I the king's knight. I honour the king but also honour the duty a parent has to his daughter. She as everyone else in this realm, has free choice," said Sir Brent.

"I Sir Damon Roth beg your indulgence in this matter and ask you to forgive my granddaughter and son in law. She will not go of her own free will that much I know. While my heart goes to her I do honour the will of the king. I yield to him and will put her in irons and cast her into a prison wagon. I will drag her in chains to his court, if that be in case what he wants."

Rhianna watched the emissary's face turn red not knowing what to say. Her foxy grandfather had beaten him at his own game, diplomacy. He looked as though he would pass out at any minute.

"I will attend the king on this matter and assure you we will return."

The entourage left in haste at full gallop as though being chased. Rhianna knew that this would not end the matter. The king would be a man of pride and would not accept her rejection. She would not go to him at his beckon and call; she would not lower herself for even king and country to the manners of a woman for hire. He would not buy her with a crown; he would have to win her favour as any other man. If she thought any less of herself then of what use would she be to him.

CHAPTER XXVI

It was a normal summer day like any other when word came to the keep that an army was marching their way. Two thousand soldiers were coming north toward Kara Keep, at the head of his troops was the king himself. Rumours told of huge catapults in tow and wagons loaded with supplies. It looked to all as though the castle was to be put under siege.

At Kara Keep the family gathered in the great hall.

"It's a show of force I believe. Who knows what the emissaries told the king," said Sir Roth.

"What do we do?" asked Brent.

"We put on our own show of force. Let the king see what he is threatening. Let him personally with his own eyes see the power of this fortress. We'll lock it down and put two hundred men inside then send the rest half a day's ride north," said Sir Roth.

"We will not fire on him will we?" said Rhianna.

"No, I hope it won't come to that. I hope he's smart enough to see he'll lose most of his army if it comes to a battle," said Sir Roth.

"Will your men stand with you against the king?" asked Rhianna.

"I'll give all an option to leave. I think some would stay.

They've made their homes here and the king threatens them as well as us," said Sir Roth.

"I will not stand for bloodshed," said Rhianna.

"It's not just about you. The king breaks his own laws. As a knight I owe loyalty to the king but also have a duty to the land and laws. It's my duty to protect those wronged and also my duty to family that outweighs my loyalty to the king," said Sir Roth.

"Let us see what he has to say before we talk of war. I believe he has been ill advised on this matter," said Amanda.

"I agree," said Sir Roth.

"I'll start shutting down the castle. Should I go out to meet him?" said Brent.

"No. I want his first image to be the keep, this fortress of nature and man," said Sir Roth.

Rhianna had faith in her grandfather, a knight in service to two kings before this one. He'd kept the peace in the north for almost three decades when all before him had failed. His health was in decline due to wounds suffered at an early age but his mind was that of seasoned commander.

Rhianna walked to the ramparts and watched as villagers fled north. She knew that the king's soldiers would steal all valuables left behind whether there was a battle or not. The poor would as always pay the highest price. Ellen drove the best horses north as all knew the commanders would take what they wanted. All would depend on talks and negotiations after the king arrived.

Rhianna knew that had she gone to the king all that was unfolding would not be taking place. She wrestled with what she had done by not obeying the Lord of the land. It would have cost her nothing but a little self esteem. She could have journeyed to his castle and paraded herself before him then dealt with him at his court. It should have been her fight and not one for everyone here.

She was spoiled living with two knights in the family; they served the law and sought justice for all. But the king was the law and she should have obeyed his will. The power of life and death was in his hands, the proof he brought with him was two thousand strong.

Rhianna was a descendant of knights, nobility, and welled with pride. Why couldn't he have left her alone? She could find her own way and did not want the crown of a queen.

Rhianna had already decided that no one would die because of her. If need be she would take her own life and end this ludicrous affair that she had caused. No one would die because of her.

Rhianna and her father rode into the valley for a final check before the castle was shut tight. They walked their horses through the valley looking for signs of life. Colby the innkeeper was still open for business. If the door was locked the oncoming soldiers would break it down and take whatever they wanted, he had a lot to loose. He would take in many coins if all the men paid. Within two days his stock would be depleted and he would have problems. Tempers would flare and they would take it out on his inn. Soldiers survived on food and ale, everyone knew that.

All the women were gone including Melanie the healer. They would not be safe young or old with two thousand drunken soldiers in town. And they would drink that first night or two after the week long march north, drink until the ale ran out and then they would turn mean.

Rhianna and her father rode through town into the fields

and the first things in sight were the sheep. There was no time to move them north and a lot would be slaughtered for food. She hoped the dogs would cower and run as any protecting the sheep they would be killed.

Rhianna saw the first soldiers and alerted her father. It was an advance scouting party of about ten men. The soldiers only stopped and stared not bold enough to move forward. Rhianna and Brent returned the soldiers stares then turned and rode toward the keep.

Rhianna focused on the sight before her and tried to imagine what the king would first see. There was a cliff the height of twenty men with a narrow stone trail winding to the top. There were mountains on both sides of the ridge where the keep sat. The mountains were rock faced and could not easily be climbed by soldiers weighted with armour and weapons. It was a natural fortress and was actually a castle in itself. Sitting on top of the ridge and flush with the edge raised stone walls four men in height. Towers twice the height of the walls stood one at each corner of the rectangular compound. Siege weapons could only be brought to the base of the cliff as the stone road was too narrow and winding to accommodate them.

Rhianna and her father rode through the front gate. It was no easy chore to open or close those wood and steel reinforced barriers. Two stout draft horses were needed to work the pulling mechanisms to open or close those gates. The large wheels and chains groaned in effort when the horses yanked them shut. Today the castle would be sealed shut which meant moving the horses' harness to another set of wheels and chains. This brought down a large iron gate, the portcullis, from above, creaking until the iron bars sunk into holes in the stone ground. If the outer wooden door was set aflame these iron gates would hold the invaders at bay.

Sir Roth gathered two hundred of his soldiers in the centre court yard.

"I believe you've all heard the rumours and know the king's army approaches and why. The north gate is still open. Any man not wanting to stand by me may leave and I will think none the less of him. My hope is that no battle will be fought this day or the next. But if we fight then we fight the king himself which will be considered treason with a punishment of death. Please choose now," said Sir Roth.

All his soldiers stood silent, no one moved. Then one voice from the back row cried out.

"I will not leave your side, Sir."

Then all two hundred as though one cried out.

"Nor I."

Rhianna watched her grandfathers lips tighten to stop the trembling and watched his eyes half shut to hold back the tears.

"Thank you. I and my family will do what we can to save us all."

At that moment Rhianna was assured she would have to do something to avert an outcome that would cost even a single life. She was powerless against so many or maybe not she thought. She would use her power as a woman, the power any woman has over a man.

Rhianna ran back to the court yard then scaled the ramparts. She watched more scouts advance into the village below, about one hundred in all. Time passed then a large column of soldiers moved toward the hamlet, a man on a white horse in the lead.

Soldiers spread left and right spilling into the fields below the keep. Supply wagons were soon in sight and not long after tents were raised, soldiers throughout the field set campfires ablaze. A large tent was erected in the centre of it all. That would be the tent of the king.

Night was filled with sounds of steel and men far below. Roars of laughter and shouts were heard until the middle of the night then silence swept through the camp. Sentries moved by the campfires through the night, the occasional sound of a sheep was all Rhianna heard; no wolves dared to howl.

Morning brought the sound of troops, wheels and iron, as two siege weapons were set into place. Rhianna joined her two knights on the ramparts as she looked to the valley below.

"Those weapons don't have the height. Thrusting rocks large enough to break down the gates they'll hit only the cliffs below. Smaller rocks that would reach the gates would not penetrate the barriers. We have nothing to fear from them. The ladders they bring are too short. It's only a show and the commanders would now advise the king of their inadequacies," said Sir Roth.

Rhianna had more than enough of the ego and pride that drove men to this course, the path of war.

"Open the gates," yelled Rhianna.

She ran down the stairs standing in front of the barriers below.

"I'll go with you," said Brent.

"No, she's her mother's daughter. Have faith. If anyone can put an end to this it is she," said Sir Roth.

The iron gates were unlocked then creaked upward. Next the wooden door groaned as though coming unhinged.

Rhianna walked alone down the long rock path to the

valley floor. Looking straight ahead her long dark hair blowing in the wind she took unhurried strides to the camps. She wore a blue dress with white trim, the sleeves to half forearm in length. Its length was almost to the ground with pleats to her waist. She had dressed to please a man and acted as though she could.

Rhianna reached the valley floor and walked toward the large tent not taking her eyes off the view. Hundreds of eyes looked her way, staring intently wondering what she would do. No one stepped out in challenge not even the personal guards at the tent.

She strolled between them to a man with dark hair and beard that had appeared from inside the tent, his eyes on her.

"Rhianna McBoden, I believe the king has accepted my invitation and is here to see me. Might that be you dear sir?"

"Yes, dear lady, I am Richard Squire, the king."

Rhianna bowed but only slightly keeping her eyes on his as she did.

"You bring rather a large escort and siege weapons perhaps to knock upon our doors."

"I come prepared to put down a revolt in progress."

"I believe you to be a victim of false council as no revolt exists unless of course I am a threat."

"I asked you to come to my court and you refused," he said in a gruff voice.

Rhianna spoke quietly so that only he could hear, "No you told me to stand in a line, which I will not do. Stand in a line and be compared to others like a prize cow. I am the daughter of a knight and duchess not the daughter of a barkeep."

Rhianna looked into his brown eyes not breaking his stare.

Knowingly she pushed him to the limit giving him only two options: hang her or concede. He dropped his head.

"Maybe I overreacted," he said in a soft voice that only she could hear.

Rhianna reached out and grasped his hand lightly. It looked as though she would not hang today. Maybe tomorrow her pride would get the better of her again and he might change his mind.

"Would you join us at the castle or will you stay in your tent another night?"

"I will gladly join you at the castle if you would please lead the way please."

Rhianna smiled at the word "please", took him by the hand and walked with him through the valley, his personal guards dropping in behind. She acted as a woman walking with an old friend. He would come through this with dignity intact as it was she who went to him with his army standing in witness of her surrender. They ascended the path to the open gate and the castle.

Once inside all soldiers and knights bowed, Rhianna moving to face him did the same.

"Please rise. I had no idea that such a great castle existed so far north. I envy you as it is more splendid than my own. I am a proud king to have you all in my service. Sir Roth has done well as commander and enforcer of the laws of this land. I have learned a lesson this day that I have a duty to serve and not only be served. I have also learned to listen to those who are loyal to me and not to judge too quickly when I am disappointed. I am a new king and beg your indulgence. Thank you for listening, one and all."

Everyone clapped hands after he stopped speaking.

Rhianna was surprised by his speech and marvelled at his humility and honesty. She took him by the hand and led him to meet the family.

The king had heard tales of the northern knights and inquired of tactics used to tame the north and drive raiders from their lands. They were becoming more than a menace on his own shores.

The great hall was quickly filled with the king and his commanders. Most of their talk was of raiders and their attempt to overtake his empire. The subject of his siege on the keep was avoided by both sides. Rhianna felt like a stranger in their midst so did not stay long. As soon as she excused herself from the table Amanda did the same.

"We will leave the men to talk about the ways of war and walk in the courtyard, now come and tell of Edward and Dorville, we have not had a chance to talk since your return," said Amanda.

"Well Edward is still single. Oh, I am sorry that was a sarcastic remark. All else is well," said Rhianna.

"I am going to tell you something that only Edward and I know, so do not breathe a word of this to anyone. Edward has been in love with a Norman duke's wife since before you were ever born. It was the reason he never came home all these years. He crosses the channel to see her. The church will not allow her marriage annulled even though her husband has never cared for her from the first.

"Her husband, the duke, has another that he loves. Early in their marriage she provided the duke with a male heir so he really does not need her. Their marriage was an alliance and nothing more. So Edward has someone just so you know. He is always been madly in love with her. They have a child, a young woman, Chantelle. She is your age and has been a secret of theirs. The duchess pretends it's a child she adopted when a maid of hers died leaving her abandoned." explained Amanda.

"That's so sweet. I'm glad you told me and no I'll not tell a soul. You mean to tell me Clorisa and Damon don't know?"

"Oh child Clorisa and I are like one, what I know so does she but Damon and Brent don't. Edward would be furious if a man knew of this. You know men when they drink they tend to joke about personal things and she is so special he would take no teasing about her," said Amanda.

"Can I talk of it to Edward?"

"Yes, he would like it if you knew I'm sure. You visit him so often and he loves you so."

They spent the rest of the day talking and breaking barriers they had made, the kind that keeps people apart.

"Why are you all of a sudden talking to me like this, I'm sorry but have to know?" asked Rhianna.

"Brent came to me for advice as soon as he got to the keep. What he told me of your conversation with him of Morgana made you appear so grown up and wise. I realized that you were no longer a child and decided to share some family things with you. You will be taking over at the keep someday when I am gone so there are matters of which you should know. You are becoming my equal in ways foreign to me but I respect your manner and you," said Amanda.

Rhianna had nothing more to say after that and after minutes of silence they bade each other good night.

She saw Richard first thing the next day with only one of his commanders in tow.

"Would you care to show me around your country this fair day," said Richard.

"I would love to but you had better know how to ride as I do," said Rhianna with a teasing voice, a challenge to him.

They thundered their horses north into the vast forests Richard had never seen. Into the valleys and mountains that made up his kingdom. He was the first ruler to ever know these northern lands. They rode through only a fragment of the countryside then the setting sun drove them home. His commanders were nervous when he left with only Rhianna and would surely send out search parties if he were gone after dark. He was a king but with less freedom than any peasant in his realm, a prisoner of his title and crown.

Two days passed quickly as Rhianna rode with Richard and showed him more of their land. She liked the man as he was warm and friendly and lacked the arrogance of his emissaries. He was a handsome man and even without a crown would attract the ladies but saw no signs that he enticed them in any way. Rumours were rumours and this man was no womanizer from what she could see and considered him a friend.

In the middle of the third day three messengers came through the front gate, one wounded. During his absence Norland raiders came ashore by the thousands and captured his eastern lands of Camria including the royal palace. All those that could do so escaped to Dorville. The Norland army was now moving toward that castle. Rhianna worried about her uncle and his small force against the overwhelming odds moving his way.

Richard looked as though he was in shock and stared at the table before him. With a small voice of self pity he ordered his troops south in defence of Dorville. His commanders scrambled from the great hall and prepared to break camp.

As quickly as they had come, one thousand were gone. The king would leave a thousand behind and not commit all at this time. King Richard and his army moved south to stop the Norlanders who had seized his lands. They'd left everything as it was before they came. No houses or stores were looted and no sheep slaughtered. The barkeep was paid for ale the soldiers drank; they acted like enforcers of the law not an invading army.

CHAPTER XXVII

Sir Roth and his soldiers had been ordered to defend the north unless further orders arrived. One thousand soldiers would also stay at the keep; the king wanted his forces split until he further evaluated the threat. Rhianna made the decision to ride south with the king as she worried of Uncle Edward. The decision was made and no one attempted to change her mind.

Brent her father would ride along but only to the road leading west to Morland. The king had asked he assess the state of that western land and report back to him. With luck Rhianna and the king would be at Dorville, they would drive the Norlanders out.

Rhianna rode at the head of the army beside the king at his request, her father and a commander directly behind. Their pace was fast, leaving the wagons and siege weapons at Kara Keep.

Their horses side by side Rhianna kissed her father good bye and he rode west to Morland four soldiers close behind. The rest rode south toward Dorville a storm brewing overhead.

Rhianna's skin was goose bumps as a sick feeling grew inside. The sky turned almost black before her eyes as lightning came to ground all around. She pulled her horse to the side of the road and stopped to stare into the sky. A bolt of lightning flashed hitting four soldiers; their horses stumbled to the ground. Was it an omen of things to come? Rhianna just stared as shivers ran through her at the sight.

The army was close to the enemy and would stop to prepare. All were to dismount and gather for orders from the king.

"The enemy is not far away. They are hiding near the crest of a hill a short distance from here. They stand between us and the troops at Dorville. Their plan is simple defeat us then besiege the castle. We will turn west and then southeast in hopes of making it to the castle. There we will join the five hundred troops and drive out the invaders."

The Norlanders were a superstitious bunch of heathens at times believing in demons and magic. Morag was witch they believed could see the future, not only see it but bend it her way. Listening to her they had so far won half of this land and were about to take the rest. They followed her with no exception as did King Rodak of the north. The invaders were his and he would personally disembowel any man who did not obey the witch giving Morag the power of a king.

Rhianna rode to the crest of the hill where the Norlanders hid slightly west of the main group. She could see Morag looking north and hoped she continued to do just that.

It was first heard, and then seen as one thousand soldiers raced toward the castle. Morag ordered her Norlanders to attack and so they did with blood curdling shouts and screams.

The soldiers were at the gate waiting for it to open, men pounding upon it. No one would ever know what happened that day when everything went wrong. For some reason, maybe poor command within the castle, the gates remained shut. Someone may have waited for word from a commander that never came, maybe someone was drunk. Whatever the reason the gates stayed shut forcing King Richard to lead his men into battle outnumber three to one.

The mounted soldiers met the warriors on foot. It was a though two walls with spears collided killing a hundred on contact. Rhianna watched the king slash at the raiders as his men surrounded him trying to keep him safe.

King Richard was pushed out to one side of his men leaving an opening for three Norlanders to move on him. Rhianna watched as he cut and slashed but knew sooner or later the king would be theirs. Richard was knocked from his mount not far from her. A sword cut into his arm then his side. She struggled toward him avoiding swinging swords and spears then was with him.

Richard was unconscious but alive. She struggled removing his armour and asked his men to put him up on her horse. Morag was coming their way. Rhianna mounted behind the king and rode toward the castle, the gate still shut. Morag and two hundred men ran to block Rhianna's way standing to barricade the castle. Rhianna rode from the chaos hoping she could at least save the king.

Rhianna watched from the top of the hill as the fool who commanded the castle guards made the final mistake. He opened the gates and ordered his troops out to aid the king's men being slaughtered before his eyes. It was too late as most of the king's men were gone. They too would share their fate thought Rhianna as tears flowed. Fifteen hundred men and a castle would be lost in half a day. She could do nothing but hopefully save the king. Things happened too quickly in war and this was her first battle. She hoped it to be her last.

Rhianna turned from the fighting and fled toward Mervin

castle the family summer retreat as Richard hunched bleeding in the saddle before her.

A hamlet between the two castles lay ahead. Rhianna scoured the roads for the sight of enemy troops but found none. The warriors would take the castle and fight over the spoils. That would probably take a couple of days so reasoned she would be safe for awhile.

Rhianna rode into the village and to the inn looking for a healer inside. She said only that her friend had been wounded and robbed by raiders not wanting to give away the fact that he was the king. Men at the bar carried Richard into a room and a healer soon arrived.

"He's lost a lot of blood but he's young and will probably survive," said the healer.

"Good, I want you to spread the word that raiders will come this way. Dorville castle will be taken today," said Rhianna.

"What? There's an army at Dorville."

"A bigger one defeated it."

"I have family near."

"So do I," sobbed Rhianna.

The healer sobbed as well then concentrated on her patient.

"He shouldn't ride for a week. He'll start to bleed again."

"He has to. The raiders seek all soldiers and he is one."

"I'll get what you need to see him through but know if you move him he may die."

Rhianna further tended his wounds using tricks Clorisa had taught her. She mixed special herbs, applied them to his wounds then stitched them and bandaged them tight. He would have to ride and heal at the same time, no other choice was theirs.

Rhianna purchased another horse, the best in town or so the man said. Every horse he had sold in his life was probably the best in town at the time. She met the healer who had brought her what was needed.

As night came Rhianna was unable to stop herself from dozing off. Almost dawn she woke with a jump and looked about but nothing threatened. Then Richard woke.

"What happened?" he asked.

"We will talk of it later, for now can you walk with my help?"

"I do not know but I will try. Where are my men?"

"We will talk of it later. Right now we have to ride."

Rhianna helped him to his feet and struggled to hold him upright. She made the way toward the stable and fought to help him into the saddle. She'd already loaded the supplies and had paid their way the previous night. They rode from the village and hoped Mervin castle was still free.

CHAPTER XXVIII

Rhianna squinted as she stared at the castle before her eyes seeing no signs of life, friend or foe. The village had been safe so she ventured forth hoping the same for Mervin castle was true. A guard finally challenged her so she pleaded help for a wounded soldier. Richard was almost unconscious again bending over the saddle and groaning at times.

The commander eyed them with suspicion. It was a small garrison consisting of only forty men changed often with the troops at Dorville. Toby the cook recognized her as she had been here twice and finally cleared the way. The soldiers took Richard and put him to bed. She spoke to the commander inside.

"Dorville castle has been taken. Fifteen hundred men died before my eyes. A thousand were troops of the king."

"And the king? Was he with them?"

"Yes, I rescued him and this is he. I do not want you to attempt to protect him. He has a better chance with me alone. Forty men will only attract attention and will not stand a chance against the force that will search for this man."

"But if he is the king it's my duty to defend him with my last breath."

"And that is exactly what will happen if you ride with him.

He will be taken and tortured so please do as I ask. He will tell you so himself when he wakes."

"What am I to do?"

"Take yourself and the others north, far north to Kara Keep. It will be safe there."

"And what of you?"

"I will not tell you my plan as if captured you will be forced to tell."

"I understand. Are you sure Dorville is lost. I have a family in the village not far from the castle."

"When I left the front gate was opened by some fool and they were outnumbered more than four to one. Only the castle guard remained in the fight. The raiders will come here without doubt."

Rhianna removed the dressings from Richard's wounds and cleaned them then coated the bleeding cuts with an herbs and tar to make the blood clot. She bandaged them tight as possible. She wanted to think and fought sleep but lost the battle.

Rhianna was shaken awake at the first light of dawn by the cook. She'd fallen asleep at sundown and awoke at sunrise and was still groggy from strain of the last few days. Richard woke at Rhianna's side. She had spent the night in bed with the king.

"Now will you tell me where my men are?"

"All dead."

It was all she said as he pondered the thought probably searching his memory for more.

"Did they not get into the castle?"

"No, they died outside and when the castle guard came out to help, well they would also be slaughtered."

Rhianna started to cry and went numb.

"It all happened so fast. All I could do was to save you from them," she sobbed.

"The way I feel right now I wished you had left me to die."

"You have more than a thousand men at Kara Keep. I hope the Norlanders follow and attempt to take that stronghold. It will be their end if they do, but first we must get back."

"Are we going to run for it?"

"No, you are in no shape for that, you would be dead in two days."

"What then?"

"We make our way to Morland. I have heard there is an old trail north from there. It has not been used in sometime but father told me it exists."

"The road west will probably be watched."

"Then we go through the old wood."

They quickly ate and readied to ride, the road west not far away. Rhianna felt refreshed after a badly needed night's sleep, the first in days. They mounted, Richard looking somewhat stronger sitting astride his horse. Tonight they would have no bed to sleep in and no roof over their heads. A packhorse would slow them so they took none. They would have dried beef and sleep in a blanket under the stars at night. It would have been romantic if it was not for the fact they were being chased by three thousand warriors led by a crazy old witch. Life never quite turns out the way you want it to thought Rhianna.

Rhianna looked over her shoulder on leaving the castle and saw the soldiers and staff mounting their horses. They would be able to move fast staying ahead of the masses that were sure to follow. Dorville was rich with spoils of war and would cause fighting amongst the warriors for the richest prize. Sooner or later though Morag would get the mob under control and the search would begin. The first road they would block would be the road north and the second would be the one west. The east they already had so would not bother with that and south was the sea.

Rhianna moved west on the shaded road to Morland looking for signs of Norlanders on the way. She told the king to walk his horse at a normal pace. He was to listen and look for signs of warriors to the rear. There was an army behind her looking for both of them, they would have to stay alert and if anything a little tense or they would die surely as the fifteen hundred two days earlier.

Rhianna waited for Richard to catch her as she looked for a place to rest. To the side of the road, hidden behind some trees a meadow glistened in the sun. They let the horses graze and ate bread with salt beef then washed it down with warm water from a water skin.

Rhianna looked up and down the road but saw nothing. She hoped they were far enough off the beaten path not to be seen. She glanced at the horses grazing, concealed by the foliage. She looked all around and strained to hear, nothing neither seen nor heard but the sounds of nature, the sounds of frogs, insects, and birds.

They led their mounts toward the road and were about to break cover when in the distance they heard the thunder of horses. They ran deep into the woods from where they came then peaked through the leaves of the surrounding trees. One hundred mounted warriors raced west. Rhianna felt a great burden descend on her as the enemy now had control of the road. She let out a grunt of disgust and shook her head as their options dwindled.

She remembered her father's words, the first he had told her to recite out loud when times grew lean.

"Think not of the problem only of the solution," she said.

"What?"

"My father always told me that when the world overwhelms then think not of the problem but of the solution. In that way you become a person of answers not despair," she said.

There was no hurry now so she could let Richard rest and tend to his wounds. They had lost the edge of being ahead and stealth mattered more than speed. They moved further into the bush and found a small meadow with a stream cutting through it.

"So what is the solution?" asked Richard.

"We cross the road and find a way through the woods."

"It will be a long walk."

"For me you will sit on your horse while I lead."

"Oh no, I will walk."

"You will slow us down, now lean back so I can clean your wounds."

Rhianna pulled off his shirt but he objected to her removing his pants.

"Who do you think put the dressings on your thigh in the first place? Now come on silly, I have to clean and check it."

He was reluctant but did comply letting her remove his pants and dressings. Rubbing the inside of his thigh with a cloth did arouse him.

She smiled as he was definitely embarrassed. She dressed the wounds then washed her hands in the stream.

Rhianna decided a day's rest was the least Richard needed. He was still bleeding despite the clotting herbs she'd administered. The stitches were holding and his wounds were healing from inside out as they should. If she could keep him from tearing anything open in the next few days he would be over the worst.

They carefully crossed the road hiding their trail. She helped Richard into the saddle then tied the reins of his horse to the stirrups of hers and led the two through the dense bush. She risked following dear paths knowing a bear could be waiting around every turn. Richard had to ride lying flat on his stomach as the low branches tore at his wounds.

When the sun hovered close to the horizon near the end of day she looked for a meadow to no avail. They sat backs against a tree chewing on dried beef and hard bread. The horses picked over what little foliage they could find then laid down between the trees going to sleep for the night.

"How long do you think it will take us?" asked Richard.

"I do not know, we are moving so slow and half the time we are going in the wrong direction avoiding swamps or dense growth. We will zigzag our way there sooner or later."

"Do you think our soldiers have reached the keep?"

"No, not yet, not for a couple of days."

"I hope they do not send troops south."

"Grandfather will not let anyone leave when he hears of the enemy's strength. He will know the best chance they have got is to stay at the keep."

"Do you think the Norlanders will siege the keep?"

"I believe they would be fools to leave such a stronghold sitting untouched at their backs. I think they will try to take it."

"I am the king and ask strategy. It is I who should know."

"You are right, you should. But then we are just making conversation, are we not?"

"I think more of Morag's own will die than ours if she attacks Kara Keep," said Richard.

"The witch leader does not care. Just as long as she gets what she wants."

"Death for the sake of profit seems cold and makes me shudder," said Richard.

"All death makes me shudder."

CHAPTER XXIX

Days passed as they wound through the woods then suddenly the soggy fields of Morland lay before them. Rhianna scanned the rolling countryside for familiar markers, soon finding one. Welton castle was over a day away. They would have to locate a place to spend the night. She didn't think they would encounter any Norlanders here being far from the main roads. Rhianna wondered about the invaders she had seen on the road heading west. They would be well into Morland by now and could surface anywhere. The castle guard consisted of only fifty men so would not be a large force to overcome. It would take more than a hundred to lay siege to the tiny fortress. Her mother and father had defended it against more than that years ago.

Anxiety raced through Rhianna as she stared at Welton castle by the waning light of day. Over one hundred Norlanders were laying siege to the castle and more were probably coming their way. Rhianna wished she had the heart of a warrior, her mother Morgana would know what to do.

They dismounted and walked their horses to a grove of trees. In the last light of day Rhianna checked and bandaged Richard's wounds as tightly as possible without cutting the flow of blood. They lay together on blankets talking of nothing in particular to pass the time. In a low voice Richard told of his strict upbringing and daily practice with weapons and horses.

Richard's first battle was fought seven years ago at the age of nineteen and his second less than a day later. He became king after watching his father die in a battle with the Norlanders less than two years ago. She heard of advisors pushing him to wed so that he'd have a male heir. She'd heard of the line up he'd refused to interview. Then she heard of the tales his advisors spread about her refusal to come to his court. They said a revolt was in progress and a show of strength would be needed to put it under control.

Rhianna didn't believe him knowing there was more to the story than that. He had probably ridden north with the intention of intimidating her grandfather and his troops. Seeing Kara Keep turned the tide as he was the one being humbled and not them. That's why he backed down so quickly when she came to him at the start of his siege. There was nothing else he could do. This king was a handsome persuasive diplomat that day at the keep. He was not a stranger to playing with words but in this case was a liar.

Richard knew the Norlanders and their customs.

"Tomorrow I will challenge the leader man to man. Believe me when I say that if I kill him they will go to the coast and bury him at sea. They will get drunk in his honour and feast for two or three days. It will give us time," said Richard.

"And if he kills you, your wounds are still not mended. You cannot do it."

"I have to there is no other way. If I do not all in the castle will eventually die. We have to get them out of there and north. They are my people as much as yours."

"We will see in the morning."

The next morning Rhianna saddled the horses by the light of the rising sun. Its brightness made it impossible to see east so they would not be seen until they arrived at the invader's camp.

"How are your wounds, would you like me to check them before we leave."

"It matters not the state of my wounds or what you find. I do what needs to be done in service to my people. Let us not waste any more time dear lady."

Rhianna reached for him and kissed him on the lips long and sweet.

"For both of us my lord."

She rode toward the enemy camp then stopped at the edge of the horde.

"I look for your leader."

A big man moved from a tent at the centre of camp and pushed his way through the warriors as though they were but branches of trees. He would be the leader.

"What do you want with the leader?"

"It is not I but Richard Squire the king who wants to speak with you or rather challenges you I think he said. He said you would never agree as you would never leave the safety of your men. I told him I could ask that it would do no harm to ask. So I tell you now that he challenges you one on one, man against man."

"And what's the prize if I win?"

"Why the king of course. You will have the man Morag seeks."

"I accept," he said.

Rhianna waved at the figure on horse back silhouetted by the rising sun. Richard galloped toward them and dismounted as soon as he arrived, jumping clear of his horse. The big Norlander came his way and two swords rang out then came the singing of steel. The Norlander was a big man one third again bigger than the king. The power of the Raider's stroke backed Richard relentlessly while the enemy cheered on.

Rhianna's hands trembled and held tight her reins as Richard backed and even stumbling at times. He parried each stroke but was unable to thrust one of his own. Richard was totally on the defensive and looked to be weakening being knocked to his knees twice. Rhianna's lips quivered so she pressed them together tight. Richard kneeled on the ground, his sword in both hands, the point dug into the sand. The big man walked forward and stood over the kneeling king drawing his sword back for a mighty swing.

Tears flowed from her eyes, tears for the king. The big man swung his massive weight and committed all his power to the stroke. Richard at that instant slid back and rose to his feet twisting in an arc almost full circle. With sword above his head Richard swiftly struck downward, from behind the warrior, hitting the man in the back of the neck with his blade. The warrior fell with a groan and a thud, the crowd went quiet. Rhianna sat breathless waiting along with everyone else. Waiting for the big man to rise but he did not. Finally one of his own turned him over and declared he was dead.

Richard walked toward his horse and mounted, Rhianna watching every move attempting to judge his state. He'd played his part well deceiving his opponent, the big man thought him finished.

Rhianna looked toward the Norlanders carrying their leader and throwing him over the back of a horse. They were breaking camp and riding toward the coast for their ritual burial at sea.

The battle had taken place within sight of the castle and Rhianna could see small faces looking their way. They were near the gate when the cheering started for their king. Richard had challenged the Raiders, fought, and won. Rhianna's father Brent was one of the men opening the gate bowing low as Richard rode in.

CHAPTER XXX

Rhianna was at his side as the king greeted all and wasted not a minute in declaring that the castle be abandoned immediately. He hadn't even taken the time to dismount. He sat on his horse giving orders in a kind voice.

Rhianna watched as he took command and was surprised by his noble ways.

"Leave everything behind and bring only food that will last for days," said the king to all as he rode through the crowd.

"Where are we going to?" asked a woman in despair.

"To Kara Keep, our only chance," replied the king.

"I will stay and take my chances with the Norlanders," said the blacksmith.

"Then you die as all did at Dorville, to my knowledge no one survived," said the king.

"How am I going to replace what I lost?" said a woman.

"I do not know, I do not know how I am going to replace the castle I lost or the half the country for that matter but I will fight and try. Not here as here we are doomed," said the king.

"How long before we are on our way Brent?" asked the king of Sir Brent McBoden.

"Half a day I fear is the best we do as there are children and elders to ready and wagons to load."

"No wagons, we cannot be limited in the roads we choose and may have to do the same as Rhianna and I did on the way here; take a path through the woods," said the king.

"Some will not make the journey then," said Brent.

"I know and so do they but our enemy will be in pursuit within three days. They will travel at twice our pace and catch us if we do not move as fast as we can," said the king.

Rhianna approached her father and gave him a quick hug then let him return to his duties.

Less than half a day later fifty soldiers, eighty women and children made their way north. Young ones were carried and two elders lay on stretchers carted by soldiers. One hundred and thirty people on horseback and on foot fled the invaders to Kara Keep.

"Take five men and lay back Captain Bluko. Keep an eye on the Raiders and warn us if they close," said Richard.

"Brent, can you find the route north from here?" asked Richard.

"It's been ten years at least since I've travelled it and then only once. Yes, I'll find it, somehow I'll find it."

"I will go with him," said Rhianna.

"No Rhianna. We need you here to help with the children," said Richard.

Children cried and old men groaned as they walked an unbroken trail leaving all behind. Women looked back as though to say a last good bye to all they'd grown to know and love. The sun hid behind the clouds as they walked sharing their sorrow. Birds did not sing and squirrels were silent as though the world was feeling their pain.

That half day's march took its toll on the young and old as they slept even before the campfires burst into flames. No reason not to set them ablaze as no one would follow for some time. Bluko would warn them if the Norlanders were close but for now hot meals would grace the night. They had been able to bring enough fresh meat and vegetables for four days before starting into the salt beef and dry bread. Some of the soldiers gave up their mounts to be used as pack animals until the fresh rations were used. The children and elders were shaken awake so that they could eat while the stew was still warm. Rhianna watched and helped where she could. She feared one old woman would not make it through the night. Nothing could be done for her with herbs; none would replace lost youth or stave off the coming of death.

The soldiers buried the old woman at first light, the sun not coming out to say good bye. All paid their last respects as a comrade was laid to rest. Their first casualty, there would probably be more. A full day's march lay ahead as some groaned through the first steps, sore from the day before. A young girl waved to all with smile sitting on the king's lap as he rode. Soldiers let the old and young set on their horses while they led them.

The pace was faster than the day before as with nothing familiar to look back at they all marched forward with hope. They would return when the invaders were driven off, people had told Rhianna the night before. Spirits were higher today; a world lost could be regained by those with the will to try.

The rolling hills grew steeper and the grasslands gave way to dense woods. The trail was marked by Brent and his men riding ahead. The rear was still guarded by Bluko as he sent a man forward with news twice a day.

The sun was descending into the earth but not yet out of sight. Rhianna gave the little boy she was taking for a ride to his parents and rode away from the others. She galloped to a hill on the road ahead. Their journey would be slower soon with those steep hills to climb. She shook her head at the thought of the injustice the people had to face then rode back to join them.

Rhianna watched the king mount and remembered the day he had been defeated in battle. He was wounded and frail as she took him from the enemy needing to be tended. Then a week later he defeated the Norlander's leader with ease and took command of the castle guard. Richard had come a long way in her eyes since he had besieged Kara Keep out of spite for rejecting him. He was truly turning into a king.

They camped and started the campfires again; the witch knew where they were as they left a trail wide and deep, one any city raised child could follow. Another hot meal on a chilly night kept everyone warm inside.

Sunrise brought with it the first sight of that orange globe in days all bathing in its warmth. The deep woods soon shut out most of the sunlight, the path not wide at all in spots. If there once had been a road or even a trail here before it had all but grown over. The heat brought with it insects of every kind especially the little blood sucking ones. Everyone swatted, and cursed unable to avoid one of nature's wraths.

Bad news came from all directions; from the rear a rider told of a hundred mounted Norlanders in pursuit. Brent and the advance scouting party returned telling the king the way ahead was blocked, they would have to turn back and find another way.

"There's an old wooden bridge ahead that spans a gorge. It

won't hold the weight of the horses and maybe not even that of men on foot," said Brent.

"We can't go back and we can't move forward so we'll have to take a stand here and fight," said the king.

"We will be slaughtered my lord, it is more than two fighting men to one," said Rhianna.

"What do you suggest?" asked Richard.

"We will have to try the bridge, it is all we have. We cannot fight with all these children around. We will have to run the best and fastest we can," Rhianna shouted.

"You are right. Move fast, one and all and follow Sir Brent," yelled the king.

Rhianna looked at the king and saw doubt in his eyes. She followed her father to the gorge then shuddered at what she saw. The support beams were rotting and so was the wood that covered them. They would have to find a way to strengthen it, there was no other choice.

"What if we tie ropes around the beams and secure them to tree limbs above, that should give it some strength, what do you think?" said Rhianna.

"We can try it, yes it may work, we'll turn it into a suspension bridge," said Brent.

The lightest soldiers cautiously kneeled and worked their way across the creaking bridge, safety ropes tied to their waists. They ran ropes along the beams and tied them to the rotting wood then to the trees on either side above. When they finished a shaky but reasonably solid crossing lay ahead.

Rhianna swallowed hard and without a word started across with her horse's reins in hand. Her father's words of caution rang through the air when she was half way across. The right side sagged so she walked to the left leading her horse and slowly crossed. The boards spanning the beams barely held her mount's weight as they groaned and complained all the way. The ropes tightened under load. Each step the bridge made noises as though it would collapse but held fast. The wind didn't help matters as it made the bridge sway. Then stepping on solid earth she let out a sigh of relief.

Her father was next and she bit her tongue as death would be his only fate if the bridge failed. He walked his horse slowly then quickened his pace and made it as well. One by one they all made their way, the timbers groaned but held solid beneath their feet. The ropes strained especially when horses crossed. Women and children made their way next screaming in fear. They giggled with delight on the other side and smiled at Rhianna happy to be alive. Bluko and his men were the last ones to cross citing that the enemy was not far behind. They set the bridge ablaze.

The bridge's old timbers burst into flames and it quickly dropped. Rhianna stayed for a time entranced by the burning bridge knowing it had saved their lives. As she stood watching the witch Morag and a few of her warriors appeared. Rhianna looked across the gorge at her enemy. Morag sneered making Rhianna chuckle.

"Witch. You will die at Kara Keep. So follow if you dare," shouted Rhianna.

Her father beside her only stared not phased by the warriors or Morag.

"It will take them two days on horseback to get around that gorge so let's make the most of it," said Brent.

Rhianna's heart was filled with pride as her father found the grown over trail and plotted their way north. Only two days later seeing sheep grazing she knew she was home again.

The sheepdogs barked at their presence and shepherds came, wide eyed at the sight of the refugees. They followed directions given them and soon found the road north to the keep. No Norlanders were in sight and Rhianna knew they would return to the south to rejoin the main army. They would soon come to the keep.

CHAPTER XXXI

Rhianna breathed deep when she saw home again, that northern guard post on a cliff high and safe. She caught Richard and rode beside with a smile. Concern was etched deep into his face as he searched for the one thousand men he left in waiting. Rhianna remembered his orders, to stay put unless he sent word to do otherwise.

They ascended the stone path toward the front gate to the sound of the noisy wheels and chains. The gate groaned open before the king. Her grandfather stood near with a thin smile and a bow to greet Richard.

"Where is the rest of my army? I told them not to move unless instructed by me," said the king in anger.

"Don't be concerned as moving them was necessity. They are in lands just north of the keep. Grazing their horses in the same fields as sheep they would all soon run out of grass. I would not separate a horse soldier from his mount so moved the camp as well," answered Sir Roth.

Her father's eyes showed concern and winced slightly then asked, "And what of your army? There are only a few with you."

"All killed at Dorville including the castle guard, fifteen hundred men gone in half a day," said Richard not in anger but with a sour note to his voice. He said the words loud and without stop as though it was old news to him. His look was solemn avoiding everyone's stare. It was as though he were awaiting punishment or at the least criticism for his failure to command.

Rhianna broke the cold silence hanging in the air.

"We had better get Clorisa to look at your wounds before we do anything else."

Rhianna bathed for the first time since she'd left and swore she would spend the day in quiet thought under the soapy bubbles. Amanda her grandmother walked into the room and kissed her gently on the forehead. Rhianna quickly dried and dressed as sadness washed through her. The sight of Amanda brought thoughts of Dorville foremost to her mind. It was the first time in days she'd had thoughts Edward her uncle, Amanda's son. She looked into her grandmother's eyes searching for words to tell her that he was probably dead. Before Rhianna could utter a word cries of anguish overtook her.

Rhianna hugged Amanda who stood still and stiff. Rhianna knew her grandmother would not break down until she was alone. The iron lady brushed tears from her granddaughter's eyes as she calmed her with soft sounds.

"Did you see Edward die?" asked Amanda.

"No, but I heard that not a soul survived," cried Rhianna.

"We do not know that for sure, maybe he has been taken hostage, maybe he will be ransomed back to us."

Amanda stayed for only a short time and Rhianna knew that her grandmother would need some time alone. She had never been able to share pain with anyone except her husband, Sir Roth.

Clorisa and Malisa were almost finished tending the king when Rhianna walked into the room. She'd looked after him from the start so did not feel like an intruder as she gazed upon the wound on his thigh.

"Everyone should come in and take a look," said Richard his voice coated with sarcasm.

"We will have to remove those stitches in a couple of days," said Rhianna paying no attention to his tone.

"I've got to get up and move my men into position before they attack," said Richard.

"I have been thinking about that. Why move them? Where are you going to put them? There are more than enough castle guards," said Rhianna.

"I thought I would put them into defensive positions in the mountains around the keep."

"I do not know of any paths or ways to get them high enough to do any good. That is why it is so defensible because there is no way to get above it. Now listen Richard and tell me what they will see when in sight of the keep."

"Well, they will see the fortress and try to find a way to get inside."

"Will they think to be attacked?"

"Well no, it would be suicide. We are safe in here."

"My point and what if we take your men and ride through the pass a half day south and come up behind?"

"They will turn on us and due to sheer number defeat us."

"We will not stay long."

"I get the point, find a time when they will least expect it then hit and run."

"But not too fast, their mounted warriors must chase us back."

"Why?"

"We will ride through the valley where Rogun and his men will lie in wait in the hills on both sides. We will turn on them and defeat them."

"How do you know Rogun will help?"

"Because he is smart enough to know that if Norlanders occupy the keep, he will be next to fall. Besides he is loyal to Amanda; they all love her. Have you not noticed?"

"Your idea has merit so let us get started Commander Rhianna," said Richard with no sarcasm at all in his voice.

Amanda and Ellen would ride north and seek out Rogun and collect his men near the pass. Rhianna and Richard sent scouting parties south warning them that a clash with enemy was to be avoided. They at least had a plan besides trying to stop the Norlanders from crashing through the front gate. That would be like sitting in a tree hoping an angry bear couldn't climb up.

Two days later the scouts returned with the bad news no one wanted to hear. There was always hope they would not come this far north but that faded with the soldier's words. About one thousand mounted Norlanders followed by two thousand warriors on foot were at most two days south. Morag riding an ink black horse was at the head of her army. The thousand mounted troops were extremely bad news as they would be equal to Richard's horse soldiers. She could tell by the look on the king's face he felt the same.

"Do we let them settle before we hit?" asked a commander.

"Oh yes, we will let them make camp and get comfortable, that is all," answered Rhianna.

Rhianna and Richard watched from their hiding spot on a hill as the army moved by. They looked like disorganized rabble: some wore animal skins, some cloth, and some wore armour of different sorts probably taken from other soldiers they'd killed in lands far and wide. It looked as though no two men were the same height or dressed the same. Even the horse soldiers looked a sham as half led their mounts probably too sore to ride. The horses they rode were from stables to the south, their breeding was unmistakable and Rhianna knew it well. Her great grandmother had brought small spirited horses from desert lands across the seas to the south. She'd mated them to larger breeds native to this land creating a breed fast and strong.

The one thing that stood out above all else was that they were loaded down with booty, straining under the weight of ill gotten gains. Some were bent as they walked and some had swords and armour of slain soldiers tied to their horses, one had five or six swords strewn across his saddle leaving no room for a rider. Rhianna had heard that these men fought each other to the death for their possessions and status, a thing punishable by death in her kingdom. They fought each other like wolves or dogs over scraps but in battle would die in defence of another, so were these men of the north, unpredictable at best.

Even their kings fought each other for lands, property and their Dragon ships. They would not set each others ships or villages afire when they fought as destruction of property was against their beliefs. The victor by their laws and beliefs was entitled to undamaged and intact spoils. Rhianna saw this as weakness; she would destroy her own property hoping to stave off their attack. Had Rhianna the time and support she would have set the castles left behind ablaze in hopes they would not follow her destructive trail. In command she would be known as the leader who left nothing behind but fire and ash. Let them try to raise an army with nothing more than burnt offerings as a prize. She would burn everything, grain stores, and food they would leave behind, kill cattle and sheep and let them rot in the sun. Who would follow her flaming path? If she couldn't have it neither could they.

The last of the foot soldiers walked by and Rhianna waited for rear scouts to follow. There were none as reported by soldiers a short time later. Morag would never expect a force as large as hers would be attacked from behind, it was her weakness, over confidence.

Rhianna mounted and followed at a distance barely keeping them in sight. The Raiders set up camp and no rear guard was posted. They all stared in the direction of the keep appearing to be hypnotized by the sight. Rhianna thought she could probably sneak into their camp and steal food from their plates without notice. The witch and her commanders stood on a hill gazing at the fortress and planning its demise.

The king and his soldiers soon came from behind galloping toward the rear of the enemy encampment. Men lay about the camp, their armour off, preparing food on campfires, and some asleep in tents just erected. Lancers drove home their long spears then pulled out their swords and hacked at the surprised Norlanders. When enemy bows came into view Richard sounded the retreat.

Richard and his soldiers left their foes having taken more than six hundred lives. The Norlanders caught their spooked horses and saddled them, then mounted and followed. Rhianna lay back until the soldiers passed then quickly followed the king to the pass in hopes that Rogun lay in wait.

The king's troops thundered along the valley floor and were almost at the other end when waving men came into view from well chosen hiding spots. Rogun grey and bent with age managed a single hand high in the air to Rhianna who returned the greeting. Her eyes scanned the hills as she saw about five hundred men were with the old king. These were hunters who at one time or another would have to live or starve by the skill of the bow; they were the best in the land. Rhianna hoped that in hot pursuit the enemy warriors had not taken the time to strap on their armour.

Richard sat on his horse at the head of his men a distance away from the mouth of the valley. He would still be in plain view of his adversaries charging toward them. They would race his way with no regard to the hills on either side. Rhianna stood toward his left out of the way of the battle.

The Norlanders' horses were heard before seen but soon rounded a bend coming into view. Arrows rained through the skies striking men dead, most scattering in fear. A second wave of arrows followed and then a third. Richard advanced his troops after the third volley as half their opponents lay dead on the ground. The Norlanders ran for their lives. Richard ordered his men to stop not wanting to be caught in a trap himself as the one he'd just arranged for them.

Over a thousand of Morag's force was wiped out on the first day at a cost of less than three hundred of the king's soldiers. They were still outnumbered, five hundred more of the enemy than theirs. Rhianna wondered what would come next.

CHAPTER XXXII

Rhianna and Richard raced back to the keep knowing the witch would concentrate her remaining men on the fortress, especially the south gate. They entered the north gate, still open. They would evacuate to the northern woods should it become necessary to do so. They knew secrets of the keep which would make them a substantial enemy form the north if need be. They would interrupt supplies and siege the keep for years to come as Rogun had done. The cost would be enormous and not of taste to those who wanted immediate profit above all else. They would drive the invaders out if need be.

Richard was the first to notice that Rogun and his men were gone. When asked, Amanda told him to trust the old man that he would desert no one in battle.

Rhianna walked the ramparts and gazed upon the enemy. They were still outnumbered but not by much and would need little to turn the tide of battle. At a distance she saw Morag's stare matching her own and felt a chill inside.

Night came as everyone awaited the battle that would surely come with the rising sun. Everyone was on full alert. Only a fool or a dead man could sleep on a night such as this. The enemy camp was quiet, too quiet Rhianna thought. They were assuming victory to come the next day and slept well believing they had nothing to loose. If the battle didn't go their way they would simply retreat, send for reinforcements and try again another day.

Morning greeted them with sunshine and a clear sky. The enemy camp was at ease, they slowly ate then dawned armour and readied for battle. All was done with in a casual way as though preparing for a walk in the woods.

Norlanders slowly hiked toward the stone path leading the way to the keep, with full body shields held before them. With the wave of Morag's arm hundreds of fire arrows were released and hit the wooden gate. It burst into flames sending fire high to the ramparts above. Soldiers screamed and fell burning to their deaths. Sir Roth ordered the gate opened and let it burn then had the steel bar portcullis lowered to seal the gap.

Rhianna knew the wooden gate would be burned also that the Iron Gate would be lost. The warrior's full shields deflected arrows as they made their way to the iron barricade. The portcullis would soon be smashed.

Hundreds of arrows filled the sky and hit the warriors on the stone path causing them to fall over the edge to their death. The arrows came from the mountain on their right. The Raiders turned their shields to block the next volley coming their way. Turning their shields toward the mountain left the Raiders open to the archers on the ramparts. They were surrounded as Rogun and his men fired from high in the mountain near the keep. The old man must have known a trail through those hills unknown to anyone else. His people had lived here for centuries and knew the land of their birth. Amanda had said he wouldn't let them down and that he did not do.

A few Norlanders ran from the path as others around them fell. Hundreds of warriors died before they were out of range behind the camp they'd made. Rogun and his men were high enough and had sufficient skill to hit anyone in camp so none returned.

Rhianna looked toward Rogun and his men as they fired on the enemy below. She turned to the path and watched as the wounded Raiders fell to their death from the stone trail.

The Norlanders ran leaving all their property in camp. They'd come to pillage and rape and now left their valuables behind. Their failure was complete and they wouldn't return for some time with the taste of defeat they'd suffered at Kara Keep.

The king and the soldiers cheered to Rogun and his men sitting on the mountain side. Rogun was the champion of the battles and the reason the Norlanders were defeated.

Few of the enemy caught horses so most left on foot. As they fled Richard gave orders to mount and attack, he would take advantage of their retreat. Seven hundred mounted soldiers followed them attacking the warriors as they ran. The Norlanders rallied and turned, four hundred standing ready to fight.

Richard ordered the archers forward. The bowmen took their toll against the weak shield wall; half the warriors fled leaving their shields behind. The warriors charged in defiance and so did the king's troops. They met like two walls with spears, colliding with a mighty roar. Men were no match against mounted soldiers so Richard's army triumphed with the loss of two hundred men. No prisoners were taken as the Norlanders fought to the last man, it was their way.

Rhianna rode beside Richard as they moved south with his dwindling army, only five hundred men. Farmers and hunters joined him along the way and fifteen hundred strong marched on Dorville. It was Rhianna's presence with the king of the land that attracted so many. Tales of their ventures and victories spread through the country like wildfire. The warrior king and the Rhianna were larger than life, people seeking them out with a desire to become part of the saga that would be told by bards for the next hundred years.

The castle at Dorville had been abandoned, the front gate still smashed. Farmers said the Norlanders moved east so that is where Richard went. At Dorville he received support of five hundred more men, more farmers, villagers, and thieves. They were now two thousand in all. Farmers and tradesmen seeing his peasant troops joined with what weapons they had. Men with pitchforks and axes moved east with the king and Rhianna in the lead, the numbers to great to count. Thousands marched but who could count numbers so great, the last of them were not in sight. A sea of angry men descended on the invading raiders.

The king met the Norlanders three days later with a force double that of the raiders. Campfires burned on both sides that night strange noises coming from the raider's camp. The rising sun gave proof to what spies had said; the king's enemy was gone. The Norlanders had run in the night knowing defeat would come with dawn. They were not foolish enough to fight to the last man when they had an alternative. It was also a bad omen for the raiders that their witch had deserted them in the night. Morag knew that she would be the first the king would hang.

A great weight had been lifted from Rhianna as she viewed the empty enemy encampment.

"The sad part in all of this is that they will be back," said Richard.

"They are raiders, it is the way of life for them, trying to get something for nothing as though the world owed them a living," said Rhianna.

"All we can do is rebuild and stay on guard."

The final battle was to be fought here in Richard's own lands of Camria within sight of the King's palace. The king thanked all for their help, moving through the vast army shaking hands for the remainder of the day. The army to large to feed split up and all returned home happy to be part of history of their land.

Iberness the king's castle was a mess and so it was wherever the Norlanders went. They were the dirtiest people Rhianna had ever seen, there was rubbish everywhere. The streets within the castle walls were lined with freed slaves cheering while their saviours rode by.

Rhianna stayed at court for sometime but felt as though she was in the way. She made excuses and left for home, returning to Kara Keep. Her father rode at her side again in place of the king. Rhianna smiled at him often happy that things were the way they'd used to be.

They were greeted with cheers from their loved ones at the keep; the news of victory preceded them.

Rhianna stood on the ramparts overlooking the valley and village below. She had seen Richard at home in his world, a king in every sense of the word. He had handled the politics and matters of court with expertise. All of his life was foreign to her. The king needed a woman with which to share the responsibilities of rebuilding a country. That certainly was not her. She was not the wallflower to fill a life at court; the daily rituals to her were a bore. She was her father's daughter, a traveller with a need to be free and a desire to be of help to others not only herself.

Above all there lay the stigma of what happened the day he laid siege to Kara Keep. Only he knew what had transpired, all she knew was that everything he'd said about the matter was a lie. Richard had come north expecting all to fold in his wake, in fear of the king and his vast army. She believed that pride and ego ruled that day not bad advise. Richard had almost lost his kingdom over that mistake. And who had he to thank for saving it? The ones he was about to wrong for his young arrogance as a king. Rhianna had saved the life of a man that threatened her freedom and free will. She saved the life of a man that would have enslaved her if she and others had not stood in his way. Richard Squire had a lot to live with, an unjustifiable mistake and the rule of a country under siege. Richard did not need her at his side reminding him of that every day of his life.

As for Rhianna she had two knights at her beckon and call. What else would a young woman need?

CHAPTER XXXIII

Amanda walked toward the front gate leading Ruby a descendant of Sapphire. Damon Roth, her husband and always first knight, followed. A contingent of twelve soldiers waited for them at the gate.

"Rhianna, look after things while we are gone. You are the Lady of the castle now," said Amanda.

"I want to go along. I will fret all the time you are gone," said Rhianna.

"No Rhianna, someone of the family has to stay and command. It is for me and Damon to do. Edward was our son. Either he was killed at Dorville or not. In any case we will go to the land of the Normans and see his love and his child. It is for us to do and no one else."

"May the Gods look after you," said Rhianna.

Amanda and Damon rode through the front gate then down the winding path to the village below. People were cleaning up debris and spoils left by the raiders. They would be paid for their inconvenience this time. That was rare. Peasants were usually at the loosing end during war. This time they had everything from jewellery to swords to sell, the first time most had more than the clothes on their backs. Today they were rich.

Amanda had not left the valley for many years, no reason

to. A horse and rider were coming their way at full gallop. It was Ellen.

"Good morning. Mind if I ride with you a ways?" said Ellen.

"Good morning. Where are going to?" asked Amanda.

"Dorville. It has been years since I've seen the place."

Amanda looked at Damon who only smiled. Over thirty five years ago Amanda had taken Ellen to Dorville to fetch sheep for Kara Keep. Her company would bring to mind a lot of memories both good and bad.

"All right. Come along if you can keep up," said Amanda.

"I'll try."

Ellen known long ago as the Princess of horses rode ahead.

Amanda looked left and right at the sheep grazing the hills. It was late morning, the sun high, only a few puffy white clouds in the sky. The grass glistened still wet from the morning dew. The sound of sheep and the barking of herding dogs were all around. The air was fresh with the scent of wild flowers and animals. That's why Amanda never left the valley, there was no place more beautiful on earth.

It seemed as though the sun refused to set as it sent rays of light through gaps in the surrounding trees. They made camp, the soldiers hunting for dry wood. Amanda sat on a log tired from the long day of riding, something she'd not done for many years. She wondered why she rarely ventured into this beautiful world. Why sit inside?

She'd spent most of her time on paper work, balancing and calculating ledgers. Letters had to be sent, people paid for their labours, and money had to be earned to balance it all out. And with the recent war, well that was another matter. It left her treasury almost bare supporting the King. Where was she to get the money to see everyone through another winter? Few people were buying as everyone was in the same position as her.

With all the problems she had, all the work that lay ahead, there was one thought that loomed over everything else in her life. Where was her son, Edward? Was he killed defending Dorville? If so then someone would know. Someone somewhere had to know something one way or another. She glanced at Damon knowing he felt the same way as her. He smiled in return acknowledging the feelings she had.

Daylight had all but disappeared when Ellen rode into camp. Amanda smiled knowing that the woman was worth more than their four army scouts. She was like the right hand of Mother Nature looking after everything that lived. Amanda could never remember seeing her sleep. For some it would be a lonely life, walking in the dark all night tending sheep. Ellen had told her there was no other life for her. Amanda feeling safe and sound soon fell asleep.

Someone wouldn't stop shaking her so Amanda finally rose. She hadn't slept so soundly in years. She staggered to the fire and nibbled a few pieces of bacon. The sun was barely above the trees, white clouds in the east, the rest of the sky clear.

The day passed without event but not the night. Dark clouds formed in the evening and burst overnight. Now Amanda remembered why she'd not left the valley and stayed within a day's ride of the keep. It was one of those torrential summer rains that almost drowned her. The air was heavy, it was hard to breathe. It didn't clear in the morning and continued to rain all day. It was as though there was a direct pipeline from the sea to here.

Three more days in the mud and rain then finally it was there, Dorville castle. A warm dry bed and a hot fire awaited her.

They entered the front gate and were immediately challenged by soldiers.

"Who are you and what is your business here?"

"I am Amanda Daggot, the Duchess and owner of this castle. Who are you?"

"Stay here. I will get the commander."

It seemed like and eternity that they sat on their horses in the drizzle then finally the soldier returned with the commander. Amanda could almost feel the warmth of the hearth. A few more minutes and they'd have this all straightened out. She was home at last.

"I am Amanda Daggot as I told your man here. Please stand aside so that I may enter my own castle."

"The castle and its lands have been confiscated by the crown for failure to pay the levy."

"What?"

"You can speak to Duke Ramsy inside if you wish."

They dismounted and Amanda followed by Damon went into the castle to see the new Duke.

The fat man sat behind her desk. That was the first and most penetrating thought that entered her mind when she saw that short bald headed excuse for a man sitting in her chair. Amanda's patience was worn paper thin.

"What is all this about. As far as I am concerned I am on the wrong side of this desk," snapped Amanda.

"After you failed to pay the summer levy last week I made

good the sum and now own these lands, the castle, and this desk."

"We only just finished fighting a war and who drove out the raiders? Us not you."

Damon closed in on the man causing his guards to approach.

"Back off soldiers. I am a knight, Sir Damon Roth. You don't want to see me angry."

"All right, enough. I have more men than you so if you don't want to see the inside of my cells you will leave," said Ramsy.

"We will see the king and have this matter quickly attended to," said Amanda.

Amanda came here solely to find her son, one way or another, dead or alive. The arrogance of that little fat man though, she could not abide. There had to be an explanation. Having fought at the King's side only one short month ago she knew something was wrong.

They rode hard and arrived at the king's castle seeking immediate audience with him. No one knew them. Amanda looked for familiar faces but found few and the ones she found refused to recognize her. They were however given quarters and told they were being put in line to petition the king only because, as the aid put it, of their station in his society.

Two days went by then finally it was their turn to see the king, Richard Squire. They were not to go to his public court but he would see him privately.

They entered his study and there sat the king, a grin on his face.

"Good day Lady Daggot and Sir Roth."

"Good day to you your Lordship," said Amanda.

"I have been told you have a grievance concerning your lands," said the king.

"Yes, there is a man called Ramsy surrounded by your soldiers claiming my lands are his," said Amanda.

"Yes they are by my decree. You failed to pay the levy and he did."

"We did not even know it was due."

"It was posted on the front door of the castle for three days."

"We were at Kara Keep. Have you forgotten who saved your life and your country?" said Amanda trying to shame the man.

"Be careful Lady Daggot, I warn you. There were a lot of people that fought for king and country a short time ago. I cannot reward everyone and make concessions for all. Taxes had to be paid, the crown needs gold to survive and Ramsy had it. You did not," said the king.

"So what of Mervin castle and Kara Keep?"

"Mervin is also in Ramsy's hands. As for Kara Keep if you can pay the sum of five hundred pounds of silver in the next month then the castle and lands are yours otherwise you will vacate in thirty days."

"Come Amanda, we have work to do," said Damon.

Amanda did not want to go, wanted to tell the king he was nothing more than a thief. Once in the courtyard away from the king she broke free of Damon's grasp.

"So all those that did not fight. Those that stayed out of the battle and guarded their money well are to be rewarded and we suffer. This king is letting cowards buy their way into the aristocracy at the cost of those who supported him laying their lives on the line."

"I know. I feel the same as you. I was there as well remember? Kings like him do not last. He will make a lot of enemies but worst of all is the fact that no one will support him the next time the raiders come and come they will. He will be on his own with the fat man as his only support. I venture to say the little man won't even be able to lift a sword. Just picture him against the odds we defeated. What do you think?" said Damon.

Amanda laughed for the first time in a week.

"You are right. The king is nothing without us. He is only as strong as those behind him and right about now there won't be many."

They left court and hastily returned to Dorville and rented a room at the inn. They questioned farmer after farmer but no one knew Edward's fate. At a loss for further action they hired a fishing vessel to take them to the lands of the Normans.

The language being a problem they hired an interpreter. Pascal was his name and he knew the languages being a trader in both lands.

He also knew of Duke Gaspon and Lady Simone, Edward's friend. In less than a day they were at the estate requesting private audience with Lady Simone. While she waited Amanda looked to the grounds. A man with a familiar way walked through the yard with a young woman by his side. Amanda rushed out, Damon at her heels. It was Edward. Amanda jumped on him weeping, screaming his name. She hugged him tight crying in his shirt. Damon stood back and laughed.

"At least something has gone right," said Damon.

Amanda stood back and looked at her son. He had a bandage around his head.

"What happened to you at Dorville?" asked Amanda.

"I do not know and may never find out. I was fighting raiders one minute and the next woke up on a fishing boat on the Norman shore. The fisherman said some men threw me into his boat and paid him to take me across the channel. I do not even know who they were or who to thank in my prayers."

They had a lot of catching up to do but little time. Now that Amanda knew her son was alive and safe her first thoughts returned to her home, Kara Keep. The only property left of the Daggot clan.

"Will you come with us Edward?"

"Nothing to go back to from what you tell me."

"What have you here?"

"A life with Simone and my daughter Cyless."

In haste they departed the Norman lands and reunited with their troops. They returned to Kara Keep, for the time being it was still theirs. Amanda explained everything to Rhianna and Clorisa.

"Somehow I have to come up with five hundred pounds of silver or lose Kara Keep," said Amanda.

"I can easily pay that," said Clorisa.

Everyone stared at her in silence.

"Your mother gave me money to look after you should you ever need it."

"Where did you hide it?" asked Amanda.

"In a Norman bank. There is ten times the amount you need in my name. I will write a letter of release," said Clorisa.

"You had quite the mother Amanda. Was there anything she didn't think of?" said Damon.

"I wished I had left Richard Squire to the raiders that day," said Rhianna.

"No you did right. It was he who betrayed us," said Amanda.

"I always sensed there was something deceitful about him. I never trusted him, nor could I truly like the man," said Rhianna.

Clorisa was too old to ride, could barely walk these days so Brent McBoden and Damon Roth went to the lands of the Normans and retrieved the money and paid the levy on Kara Keep. Two weeks later they were back with the rest, almost ten thousand pounds of silver still left.

No one died of starvation that winter thanks to Clorisa. Thanks to all the women of Kara Keep.

THE END